For an instant the pirates pressed in close with their flashing swords but soon they fell back.

I knew their greater numbers would wear me out and eventually I would go down to certain death. I shuddered at the thought of dying in this terrible place where no word of my death could reach Dejah Thoris.

Then my old-time spirit came back. . . . I put the thought of death out of my mind, and charged my antagonists with a fury that those who escaped will remember to their dying day.

A Background Note about
The Gods of Mars

The Gods of Mars, published in 1913, is the second of a series of adventure books about John Carter, a Civil War veteran, swordsman, and polite Southern gentleman. In the first book in the series, *A Princess of Mars*, Carter finds himself magically transported to the planet Mars (or "Barsoom," as it is called in the stories). On Barsoom he meets, wins, and marries the beautiful princess Dejah Thoris. At the end of *A Princess of Mars*, Barsoom is threatened with extinction unless Carter can activate its atmosphere plant in time. The book concludes with Carter reawakening on Earth, not knowing if his efforts had been successful. *The Gods of Mars* picks up the action where *A Princess of Mars* ended.

EDGAR RICE BURROUGHS

THE GODS OF MARS

Edited by Denton Cairnes
Afterword by Beth Johnson

 THE TOWNSEND LIBRARY

THE GODS OF MARS

TP THE TOWNSEND LIBRARY

For more titles in the Townsend Library,
visit our website: www.townsendpress.com

All new material in this edition is
copyright © 2006 by Townsend Press.
Printed in the United States of America

0 9 8 7 6 5 4 3 2

Illustrations © 2006 by Hal Taylor

Townsend Press, Inc.
439 Kelley Drive
West Berlin, New Jersey 08091
cc@townsendpress.com

ISBN-13 978-1-59194-062-3
ISBN-10 1-59194-062-1

Library of Congress Control Number:
2005936426

Contents

Foreword

TWELVE years have passed since I laid the body of my great-uncle, Captain John Carter, away in his tomb.

I wondered about his instructions relating to the construction of his tomb, and especially those parts that directed that he be laid in an OPEN casket and that the bolts of the vault's door be accessible FROM THE INSIDE.

Twelve years had passed since I had read the manuscript of the adventures of this remarkable man who could not even guess his age; this man who had spent ten years on the planet Mars; who had fought for and against the green men of Barsoom; who had fought for and against the red men and who had won the beautiful Dejah Thoris, Princess of Helium, for his wife, and had been made a prince of the House of Tardos Mors, Jeddak of Helium.

Twelve years had passed since his body had been found at his cottage, and many times during those twelve years I had wondered if John Carter was really dead, or if he roamed again on the planet of Mars. I wondered if he had returned to Barsoom to find that he had opened the doors of the atmosphere plant in time to save the count-less millions on the planet. And I wondered if he had found his black-haired princess and the son he dreamed was with her.

Twelve years had passed when one evening I received a telegram directing me to meet "John Carter" at a nearby hotel. As I entered, his smile of welcome lit up his handsome face. Apparently he had not aged a minute, but was still the straight, lean, fighting-man of thirty, looking just like I remembered him, nearly thirty-five years ago.

"Well, nephew," he greeted me, "do you feel like you're seeing a ghost, or suffering from the effects of too many mint juleps?"

"Juleps, I reckon, but maybe it's just the sight of you again that affects me. You've been back to Mars? Tell me. And Dejah Thoris? You found her well?"

"Yes, I have been to Barsoom again—but it's a long story, too long to tell in the limited time I have before I must return. My heart is in Barsoom with my Martian princess and I doubt that I will ever leave her again. I have come now to give you these notes."

He patted a swelling portfolio that lay on the table at his elbow and said, "I know that you are interested and I know that the world is interested, too, though they will not believe these things for many ages. Earthmen cannot comprehend the things that I have written in these notes.

"Give the people what you think will not harm them, but do not feel bad if they laugh at you."

That night I walked down to the cemetery with him. At the door of his vault he turned and shook my hand.

"Goodbye, nephew," he said. "I may never see you again. I doubt I'll ever leave my wife and boy while they live, and the span of life on Barsoom is often more than a thousand years."

He entered the vault and the door swung slowly closed. The ponderous bolts grated into place and the lock clicked. I have never seen him again.

But here is the story of his return to Mars. There is much that I have left out but you will find the story of his second search for Dejah Thoris, Princess of Helium, even more remarkable than the first.

E. R. B.

The Plant Men

Standing by my cottage on that cold night in March, 1886, I again felt the compelling influence of the god of war, my beloved Mars. For ten lonesome years I had begged the planet to carry me back to my lost love.

Not since that other March night in 1866, when I stood outside the Arizona cave, had I felt the attraction. I stood praying for a return of the strange power that had drawn me through space, praying as I had prayed on thousands of nights before during the ten years I waited and hoped.

Suddenly nausea swept over me, my knees gave way and I fell to the ground. Instantly my brain cleared and there, across the threshold of my memory, swept the horrors of that ghostly Arizona cave. Just like on that long ago night, my muscles refused to respond to my will and I could hear again the awful moans and rustling of the fearsome thing which had threatened me from the back of the cave. I made the same superhuman effort to break the bonds of the paralysis, and once more came the sharp click, and I stood naked and free beside the lifeless thing that had so recently been my live body.

With scarcely a parting glance I turned my eyes toward Mars, lifted my hands up, and waited. It was not long before I shot into the void. There was the same instant of cold darkness that I had experienced twenty years before and then I opened my eyes in another world. I found myself beneath the burning rays of a hot sun shining through an opening in the dome of an immense forest.

The scene that met my eyes was so un-Martian that a sudden fear swept through me that I had been aimlessly tossed onto some other planet. I lay on a patch of red grass-like vegetation, and around me stretched a grove of strange and beautiful trees, covered with huge blossoms and filled with brilliant, voiceless birds. I call them birds, but the human eye never rested on such odd, unearthly shapes.

Some vegetation was similar to that which covers the lawns of the red Martians of the great waterways, but the trees and birds were unlike anything that I had ever seen before. Through the trees I could see a most un-Martian sight—an open sea, its blue waters shimmering.

As I rose to investigate I experienced the same ridiculous situation as on my first attempt to walk on Mars so long ago. The lesser gravity and reduced air pressure of its atmosphere gave so little resistance to my earthly muscles that the ordinary exertion of rising sent me several feet into the air and landed me on my face.

This experience proved to me that I might indeed be on Mars, though in some unknown area. I tried again, and soon mastered the art of tuning my muscles to these changed conditions.

As I walked toward the sea I could not help but note the park-like appearance of the grass and trees. The grass was as close-cropped and carpet-like as a lawn and the trees themselves showed evidence of careful pruning up to about fifteen feet. As I turned my glance in any direction the forest had the appearance of a vast, high-ceilinged chamber.

This appearance of careful cultivation convinced me that I had made my second entry onto Mars into the domain of a civilized people. I hoped that when I found them I would be accorded the courtesy and protection due me by my rank as a Prince of the House of Tardos Mors.

I found the trees remarkable. Their trunks, some a hundred feet in diameter, told of their tremendous height. As far up as I could see the trunk and branches and twigs were as smooth and highly polished as a fine piece of furniture. The wood of some of the trees was as black as ebony, while the nearest neighbors were white. Some others were scarlet, yellow, or the deepest purple.

As I neared the edge of the forest I saw a broad expanse of meadowland, and as I was about to emerge from the shadows a sight met my eyes that took away all romantic reflection on the beauty of the strange landscape.

To my left the sea extended to the horizon, ahead only a vague, dim line indicated its far shore, while at my right a river, broad and majestic, flowed down to empty into the quiet sea. A short distance away, the river appeared to flow out of the base of some high cliffs.

But it was not this evidence of Nature's magnificence that drew my attention from the beauty of the forest. It was the sight of a group of figures moving on the meadow near the river.

They were odd, grotesque shapes, unlike anything that I had ever seen on Mars, and yet, at a distance, slightly manlike in appearance. The larger specimens appeared to be about ten feet high when they stood erect. Their arms, however, were very short, and from where I stood seemed like an elephant's trunk, moving in sinuous and snakelike motions, as though they had no bone structure. As I watched them from behind a tree, one of the creatures moved slowly in my direction, running his oddly shaped hands over the ground.

As he approached I got an excellent view, and I must say that after one look at this freak of nature nothing could get me away from this hideous creature quickly enough. Its hairless body was a strange and death-like blue, except for a broad band of white around its large single protruding white eye. Its nose was a ragged, inflamed, circular hole in the center of its blank face; a hole that resembled a fresh bullet wound. Below this repulsive opening the face was quite blank to the chin, for the thing had no mouth.

The head, with the exception of the face, was covered by a tangled mass of jet-black hair some ten inches long. Each hair was about the size of a large worm, and as the muscles of its scalp moved, they seemed to wriggle and crawl around the horrible face as though each separate hair had independent life. The body and the legs looked almost human and the feet too, were human in shape, but of monstrous proportions. From heel to toe they were three feet long.

As it came close to me I discovered that its strange movements, running its hands over the surface of the ground, was its method of feeding, which consists in cropping off the tender vegetation with its razor-like claws and sucking it up through its two mouths, which each lie in the palm of a hand.

In addition, the beast had a massive tail about six feet long, round where it joined the body, but tapering to a flat, thin blade toward the end.

As I had been studying this monstrosity the rest of the herd had moved quite close to me. Horrible-looking as they were, I did not know whether to fear them or not—they did not seem to be particularly well equipped for fighting. I was on the point of stepping from my hiding place when I was stopped by a shrieking wail from the cliffs.

Naked and unarmed as I was, my death would have been horrible at the hands of these creatures, but at the sound of the shriek each member of the herd turned in its direction. At the same instant every worm-like hair on their heads stood out stiffly like they were listening for the source of the wail.

Every eye then turned toward one large member of the herd. A strange purring sound issued from the mouth in one of his hands. At the same time he started toward the cliffs, followed by the entire herd.

Their speed and method of movement were both remarkable, springing in long leaps of twenty feet, just like a kangaroo. They were rapidly disappearing when it occurred to me to follow them, and so, throwing caution to the winds, I ran behind them with my own leaps and bounds.

They went directly to the source of the river at the base of the cliffs. As I hid behind a series of boulders I came quite close to the cause of the disturbance before I saw what was happening. I saw the herd of plant men surrounding a group of green men and women. I now knew I was on Mars, for these were members of the wild hordes that populate the dead sea bottoms and deserted cities.

There were two men and four females standing back to back, facing the hostile actions of the plant men. Both men and women were armed with swords.

The leader of the plant men charged the little party, and his method of attack was as remarkable as it was effective. He charged to within a dozen feet of them and then, with a bound, jumped directly above their heads. His powerful tail was raised high to one side, and as he passed over he brought it down in a sweep that crushed a green warrior's skull.

The rest of the frightful herd was now circling around the little knot of victims. Their impressive leaps and their shrill, screeching purr confused their prey. As two of them leaped from opposite sides, the sweep of those awful tails met with no resistance and two more green Martians went down. There was now only one warrior and two females left.

But as two more of the plant men charged and jumped, the warrior, who was now prepared, swung his sword high and met one with a clean cut that sliced the plant man from chin to groin.

The other, however, dealt a single blow with his tail that killed both of the females.

As the green warrior watched the last of his companions go down and saw that the entire herd was charging him, he rushed to meet them. Swinging his sword, cutting to right and left, he laid an open path straight through the advancing plant men, and then ran for the forest. He turned toward the cliffs, taking the entire party away from me.

As I had watched the green warrior fight against such enormous odds my heart swelled in admiration, and acting as I tend to do, I jumped up and ran quickly toward the dead green Martians.

I was quickly at the spot, and in an instant I was in pursuit of the hideous monsters that were gaining on the fleeing warrior. This time I grasped a sword in my hand and my heart was filled with a fighting man's blood lust! I felt my lips form the smile that has always marked me in the midst of battle.

As I caught up, the green warrior stood with his back to a boulder, while the herd, hissed and screeched around him. With their single eye in the center of their heads and every eye on their prey, they did not notice my soundless approach. I was on them with my sword and four of them lay dead before they even knew it.

For just an instant they drew back from my

onslaught and the green warrior rose to the occasion. Fighting to my side he swung to the right
and left with murderous cuts. His keen blade
passed through flesh and bone like thin air and
his powerful circling strokes never stopped until
no one stood to oppose him.

As we joined in the slaughter, that shrill,
weird cry which had called the herd to the attack
was repeated. Again and again it sounded, but we
were too much engaged with the creatures
around us to check out its source.

Tails lashed around us as razor-like claws cut
our limbs and bodies. A green, sticky syrup
smeared us from head to foot. Every cut and
thrust of our swords caused this stuff to spurt
from the severed arteries of the plant men.

Once I felt the weight of one of the monsters
on my back and as sharp claws dug into my flesh
I experienced the frightful sensation of moist lips
sucking out my blood. I was fighting with a ferocious monster trying to reach my throat, while
two more were lashing at me from either side.
The green warrior was barely holding his own,
and I felt that the struggle would not last much
longer when the huge fellow saw the fix I was in.
Tearing away from those that surrounded him,
he cut the one off my back with a single sweep of
his blade and, relieved from that burden, I had
little difficulty with the others.

We moved against a boulder that kept the

creatures from soaring above us to deliver their deadly blows. Since we were more equally matched while they remained on the ground, we were making headway in killing them when our attention was again attracted by the shrill wail above our heads. This time I glanced up, and far above us stood a strange figure of a man. He was shrieking while he waved one hand toward the river's mouth and with the other pointed toward us.

A glance in that direction showed hundreds of these leaping creatures heading toward us, and with them some strange new monsters.

"It will be a great death," I said to my companion. "Look!"

As he shot a quick glance in that direction, smiled and said, "We will at least die fighting as great warriors should, John Carter!"

We had just finished off the last of our immediate attackers, and I turned in surprise at the sound of my name.

And there before my astonished eyes I saw the greatest of the green men of Barsoom; their shrewdest statesman, their mightiest general, my great and good friend, Tars Tarkas, Jeddak of Thark.

A Forest Battle

We had no time to exchange pleasantries as terrifying creatures came from all directions in response to the call of the man above us.

"Run!" shouted Tars Tarkas, "Head for the cliffs! Our only hope is to find a place where we can defend ourselves!"

We raced toward the cliffs. Once there we'd have to seek out a shelter for our stand against the plant men. Tars Tarkas yelled at me to sprint ahead and find a fighting place. Throwing every ounce of my earthly muscles into the effort, I cleared the remaining distance.

My quick inspection of the cliff could not find even a hint of a foothold. To my right the bottom of the cliff was lost in the dense foliage of the forest and to the left the cliff ran across the border of the broad valley.

A thousand feet away the river poured out from the base of the cliffs and I could see no chance of escape in that direction. I turned my attention back to the forest. Here, the cliffs towered above me several thousand feet. The sun was not quite on them and they loomed a dull yellow in the shade. Here and there they were broken with streaks and patches of red, green, and white quartz. They were very beautiful, but I did not have time to appreciate them at this moment.

Tars Tarkas was approaching me rapidly, followed by the awful horde at his heels. It seemed we'd have to choose the forest, and I was just motioning for him to follow me when the sun passed over the cliff's edge. As the sun's rays touched the dull surface, it burst into a million lights of shining gold, flaming red, soft greens, and gleaming whites—a more gorgeous and inspiring spectacle, a human eye has never seen!

The face of the entire cliff was so covered with patches of gold it looked like a solid wall of the precious metal except where it was broken by outcroppings of ruby, emerald, and diamond boulders—an indication of the vast riches buried behind the magnificent surface.

But what caught my interest the most were the several black spots that now appeared plainly across the gorgeous wall close to the top of the trees. I recognized them as the dark openings of caves—possible avenues of escape.

There was only one way to reach the caves, and that was by climbing the trees. I knew that I could climb but Tars Tarkas, with his enormous weight might find it impossible. However, we had to give it a try.

Our pursuers were now so close that it seemed impossible for him to reach the forest. The green men of Barsoom hardly ever run away from their enemies. Tars Tarkas had shown himself bravest of the brave thousands of times in mortal combats with men and beasts. I knew there was a reason other than fear behind his flight from these monsters, just as he knew that a greater power than pride or honor spurred me to escape. In my case it was love—love for Dejah Thoris. The cause of his actions I could not even guess. The Tharks more commonly seek death—these strange, cruel, loveless, unhappy people.

We reached the shadows of the forest, but right behind us was the swiftest of our pursuers—a giant plant man with his claws reaching out to fasten those bloodsucking mouths on us. He was a hundred yards in front of his closest companion, so I called to Tars Tarkas to climb a tree while I took care of the fellow. I hoped to give the Thark a chance to reach the higher branches before the horde of plant men was on us.

I did not anticipate either the cunning of this brute or the swiftness of his following pack. As I swung my sword to finish off the creature it halted its charge and my sword cut harmlessly through air. His heavy tail then swept around and knocked me to the ground. In an instant the brute was on me, but before it could fasten its hideous mouths to my throat I grabbed a tentacle in either hand.

The plant man was well-muscled and powerful but my earthly agility, in conjunction with the hold I had on him, would have given me an eventual victory. But as we strained and struggled beneath the tree, I caught a glimpse of the swarm of beasts that were almost on me.

Now I saw the other monsters that came with the plant men. They were that most dreaded of Martian creatures—the great white apes. My former experiences on Mars had familiarized me with them, and I must say that of all the fearsome and terrible, weird and grotesque animals on Barsoom, they are the most powerful and dangerous beasts.

They stand up to fifteen feet high and walk erect on their hind feet. Like the green Martians, they have a second set of arms midway between their upper and lower limbs. Their eyes are very close together, but do not protrude like those of the green men; their ears are set high, while their snouts and teeth are much like those of our African gorilla. On their head grows an enormous shock of bristly hair.

It was these apes and the plant men that I saw over the shoulder of my foe, and then, in a wave of snarling, snapping, screaming, purring rage, they swept over me.

Instantly fangs and claws were sunk into my flesh and cold, sucking lips fastened onto me. I struggled to free myself and though weighed down by their numbers, I got to my feet, where, still holding my sword, I wrought such havoc among them that for an instant I stood free.

What it has taken minutes to write occurred in but a few seconds, but during that time Tars Tarkas had seen my plight and had dropped from the lower branches to my side, and again we fought, back to back, as we had done a hundred times before.

Time and again the ferocious apes jumped in, and time and again we beat them back. The tails of the plant men lashed with tremendous power around us as they charged from various directions or leaped above our heads; but every attack met a gleaming blade. However, even the two best swordsmen in a world full of warriors could not win forever against these overwhelming numbers. These savage brutes do not know defeat until cold steel teaches their hearts to no longer beat. And so, step by step, we were forced back. At length we stood against the tree, and then, as charge after charge came against us, we moved crab-like until we were halfway around the huge trunk.

Tars Tarkas was in the lead, and I heard him yell, "Here is shelter, John Carter!" Glancing down, I saw an opening in the base of the tree.

"In with you, Tars Tarkas," I cried, but he would not go, saying that his bulk was too much for the little hole.

"We shall both die if we remain outside! Here is a chance for one of us. Take it and you may live to avenge me. It is useless for me to worm my way into that hole with this horde of demons fighting us on all sides."

"Then we shall die together, Tars Tarkas! I will not go first. Let me defend the opening while you get in, then my smaller size will permit me to slip in before they can stop me."

We were fighting furiously as we talked in broken sentences, punctured with vicious cuts and thrusts at our swarming enemy. Eventually he yielded, for it seemed the only way in which either of us might be saved from the ever-increasing numbers of our assailants, who were still swarming in on us from all directions.

"It was always your way, John Carter, to think of your own life last. But still more your way to command the actions of others, even the greatest Jeddak that rules on Barsoom!"

There was a smile on his cruel, hard face, as he turned to obey the dictates of a creature of another world—of a man whose stature was less than half his own.

"If you fail, John Carter, know that the heartless Thark, who you taught the meaning of friendship, will come out to die beside you."

"As you wish, my friend," I replied; "but go quickly now, head first."

As he dropped to the ground to force his way into the tree, the whole howling pack of hideous devils charged me. To right and left flew my blade, now green with the sticky juice of a plant man, now red with the crimson blood of a great white ape, but always flying from one opponent to another to drink the lifeblood of some savage heart.

And so I fought as I had never fought before, against such frightful odds that I cannot understand how human muscles could withstand that terrific weight of ferocious, battling flesh. With the fear that we would escape them, the creatures redoubled their efforts to pull me down. They succeeded at last in overwhelming me, and I went down and once again felt those awful sucking lips against my flesh.

But I had just hit the ground when I felt powerful hands grab my ankles, and in another second I was being drawn into the tree's interior. For a moment it was a tug of war between Tars Tarkas and a plant man—with me in the middle—but finally I got my sword into the brute and he released his hold on me just as he released his last breath.

Torn and bleeding from many wounds, I lay panting on the ground inside the hollow of the tree, while Tars Tarkas defended the opening from the furious mob outside. For an hour they attacked the opening, but finally they confined their efforts to horrid growling on the part of the great white apes, and the indescribable purring of the plant men.

At length, all but a few left us, but we were trapped inside the tree. Of course, the only outcome if we stayed would be death by starvation, and even if we were able to slip out after dark, where in this hostile valley could we hope to run?

As the attacks ceased, I took the opportunity to explore. The hollow space inside the tree was fifty feet in diameter, and from its flat, hard floor I judged that it had often been used before. As I raised my eyes I noticed the hollow space gradually narrow but far up in the dim shaft I could see a faint glow of light.

There was an opening above! If we could reach it we might make it to the cliff caves. My eyes had now become used to the subdued light of the interior, and as I continued my investigation I found a ladder.

I climbed up to find a series of horizontal wooden bars that spanned the shaft-like interior of the trunk. These bars were set one above another about three feet apart, and continued up as far as I could see.

Dropping to the floor once more, I told Tars Tarkas of my discovery. He suggested that I explore up as far as I could go while he guarded the entrance. As I climbed up the shaft I found that the ladder of horizontal bars stretched as far above me as my eyes could reach, and the light from above grew brighter.

I continued to climb until I reached the opening in the trunk that admitted the light. It was about the same diameter as the entrance at the foot of the tree, and opened onto a large flat limb. The limb's worn surface showed its continued use as a pathway.

I did not climb out onto the limb for fear that I might be discovered, but instead hurried back to Tars Tarkas. Soon we were both ascending the long ladder toward the opening above. He went up ahead and as I reached the first of the horizontal bars I pulled the ladder up and passed it on to him. He carried it up another hundred feet, where he wedged it securely. I dislodged several of the lower bars as I passed them, and soon there was no possible means to climb up from the base. We hoped this would stop any pursuit and attack from our rear.

When we reached the opening at the top, I went out to investigate. Because of my lesser weight and greater agility, I was better able to check out this pathway. The limb went up toward the cliff a few feet above the entrance to a cave.

As I got closer to the slender end of the branch it bent under my weight until, as I balanced near its tip, it moved gently down to the level of the opening. The ground was five hundred feet below and it was thousands of feet up to the top of the cliffs. I returned to the tree trunk for Tars Tarkas and together we worked our way along the limb and soon found ourselves at the cave's entrance, with a magnificent view of the valley below us.

As far as the eye could see gorgeous forest and meadow skirted a silent sea, and around it all towered the brilliant cliffs. Once we thought we saw a golden tower gleaming in the sun through the far-distant trees, but we guessed it was just a hallucination from our great desire to find civilized men in this beautiful, yet forbidding, spot.

Below us on the river's bank the great white apes were devouring the last remnants of the murdered green folk, while herds of plant men grazed on the meadow which they kept as close clipped as the smoothest lawn.

Safe from a rear attack, we decided to explore the cave, which we hoped would lead away from this horrible valley.

We advanced though a tunnel cut from the solid cliff. We had no means of making a light, so we groped our way into the darkness. We soon came to a wall that blocked our progress and I found what appeared to be a door. Gently pressing in, I felt the door slowly give way and we looked into a dimly lit, empty room.

I swung the door wide open and, followed by the huge Thark, stepped into the chamber. As we stood for a moment in silence, gazing around the room, a slight noise caused me to turn and I saw the door swing shut. My fingers clawed at the unyielding portal, while my eyes sought some means to open it.

And then a cruel burst of laughter rang through the desolate place.

The Chamber of Mystery

After that awful laugh stopped reverberating through the room, Tars Tarkas and I stood in tense silence. But no other sound broke the stillness, nor did we see anything move. Tars Tarkas laughed softly—it's the way of his people when they are in the presence of the horrible or terrifying. It is not a hysterical laugh, but rather the genuine expression of pleasure they get from the thought of combat with something that terrifies other men.

I looked up at the Thark, a smile on my own lips, and asked, "What do you make of it? Where are we?"

He looked at me in surprise and asked, "Where are we? You tell me, John Carter. I am on Barsoom is all that I can guess, but if I had not seen you and the great white apes I would not even guess that! The other sights I have seen are as different from my beloved Barsoom as night is to day."

"Tars Tarkas, I do not know where we are on Barsoom."

"Where have you been since you opened the doors to the atmosphere plant years ago, when all Barsoom was dying? Your body was never found, though the men of the whole world sought you for years. The Jeddak of Helium and his grand-daughter, your princess, offered such fabulous rewards that even princes of royal blood joined in the search. There was only one conclusion to reach when all efforts to locate you had failed. We all thought that you had taken the long, last pilgrimage down the River Iss, to wait in the Valley Dor on the shores of the Lost Sea of Korus for the beautiful Dejah Thoris, your princess.

"Why you had gone there no one could guess, for your princess still lived—"

"Thank God," I interrupted him. "I did not dare ask you, for I was afraid I might have been too late to save her—she was almost lifeless when I left her in the royal gardens so long ago. She was so weak that I barely hoped to reach the atmosphere plant before her spirit fled from me forever. And she is alive?"

"She lives, John Carter."

"You have not told me where we are," I reminded him.

"We are where I expected to find you, John Carter . . .

"You know that it was left for a man from

another world—for you yourself—to teach this cruel Thark what friendship is; and I thought that you, my friend, roamed the care free Valley Dor.

"So I hoped the person I most wanted to be with was at the end of the long pilgrimage. As the time elapsed that Dejah Thoris had hoped might bring you back to her side—she believed you temporarily returned to your own planet—I at last gave way to my great yearning. Just a month ago I started on the journey, and today you have witnessed the journey's end. Do you now understand where we are, John Carter?"

"That was the River Iss, emptying into the Lost Sea of Korus in the Valley Dor?" I asked.

"Yes, this is the valley of love and peace and rest to which every Barsoomian since time began has longed for at the end of a life of hate and strife and bloodshed. This . . . this . . . is Heaven."

His tone was cold and ironic; its bitterness showed the terrible disappointment he suffered. Such disillusionment, such a blasting of life-long hopes and aspirations, such an uprooting of age-old tradition would have brought on a different reaction from a lesser man.

I laid my hand on his shoulder and murmured, "I am sorry." There did not seem to be anything else to say.

"Think, John Carter! Think of the countless numbers of Barsoomians who have taken the pilgrimage down this cruel river since the beginning of time, only to fall into the clutches of the creatures that attacked us today.

"There is an old legend that once a red man returned from this place. The legend has it that he told a fearful story of horrid brutes that inhabited a valley of wondrous loveliness. These brutes pounced on each and every Barsoomian as he finished his pilgrimage and devoured him right on the spot. Where the pilgrims hoped to find love and peace and happiness they found fear and torment and death. The ancients killed this blasphemer who spoke against their religion, and now tradition demands that anyone who returns from the River of Mystery must be put to a horrid death.

"But now you and I know that the legend is true, and that the man told only of what he saw. What good would it do us to escape, since even if we made it back to the outer world we would be treated in the same way and be put to a horrible death? We are between the wild thoat of certainty and the mad zitidar of fact—we can escape neither."

"As Earth men say, we are between the devil and the deep blue sea, Tars Tarkas," I replied and I could not help but smile at our dilemma.

"There is nothing that we can do but take things as they come. We will have the satisfaction of knowing that whoever eventually kills us will have far greater numbers of their own dead in the bargain. White ape or plant man, green Barsoomian or red man, whoever takes the last toll from us will know that it is costly to wipe out John Carter, Prince of the House of Tardos Mors, and Tars Tarkas, Jeddak of Thark."

I could not help but laugh at his grim humor, and he joined me in one of his rare laughs of real enjoyment. This was one of the things about this fierce Tharkian chief which marked him as different from the others of his kind.

"But what about yourself, John Carter," he asked at last. "If you have not been here all these years where have you been, and why are you here today?"

"I have been back to Earth. For ten long Earth years I have been praying and hoping for the day that would carry me back once more to this grim planet. I feel a bond of love for Barsoom, with all its cruel and terrible customs. All this time I have been worrying about Dejah Thoris, and now that my prayers are answered I find myself stuck here where there is no escape."

As we talked I had been searching the immense chamber. The walls and ceiling were the same material as the cliff, showing mostly dull gold in the dim illumination of a small light in the ceiling. Here and there polished surfaces of ruby, emerald, and diamond showed through the walls and ceiling. There was another door in the opposite wall and since we knew one was locked I approached the other.

As I extended my hand to try and open it, that cruel and mocking laugh rang out again, so close to me that I involuntarily pulled back. And then from the far corner a hollow voice chanted: "There is no hope, there is no hope! The dead do not return, the dead do not return! Hope not, for there is no hope!"

Though our eyes instantly turned toward the direction of the voice, there was no one in sight, and I admit that the hair stood up on the back of my neck.

Quickly I walked that way, but the voice stopped before I reached the wall, and then from the other end of the chamber came another voice, shrieking: "Fools! Fools! Do you think you can defeat the laws of life and death? Would you cheat the mysterious Issus, Goddess of Death, of her just dues? Did not her ancient River Iss, carry you at your own request to the Valley Dor? Do you think that Issus will give up her own? Do you think you can escape from where only a single soul has fled in all the countless ages?

"Go back the way you came, to the merciful jaws of the children of the Tree of Life or the gleaming fangs of the great white apes, for there lies a speedy end to your suffering. Continue to wander through the mazes of the golden cliffs, and death in its most frightful form will take you!

A death so horrible that even the Holy Therns, who conceived both life and death, will shield their eyes from its terror and close their ears to your shrieks. Go back, O fools! Go back the way you came!"

And then the awful laugh broke out from another part of the chamber.

"Most uncanny," I remarked, turning to Tars Tarkas.

"What shall we do?" he asked. "We cannot fight empty air. I would rather return and face foes whose flesh will feel my blade and know that I am selling my carcass dearly."

"If, as you say, we cannot fight empty air, neither can empty air fight us. I, who have faced thousands of warriors and blades, will not be turned back by wind; and neither will you, Thark!"

"But unseen voices may come from invisible creatures who wield invisible blades," answered the green warrior.

"By my sword, Tars Tarkas! Those voices come from someone as real as you or I. Their blood can be spilled as easily as ours, and the fact that they remain invisible is the best proof that they are mortal; and not even brave mortals at that. Do you think I will fly at the first shriek of a cowardly foe who will not come out into the open and face a good blade?"

I had spoken in a loud voice so our tormenters could hear me, for I was tiring of this game. I was sure this was a plan to frighten us back into the valley to be killed by the savage creatures. For a long period there was silence, then a soft sound made me turn to see a large monstrous banth creeping up on me.

The banth is a fierce beast of prey that roams the hills surrounding the dead seas. It is almost hairless with only a bristly mane around its thick neck. It has a long, thin body supported by ten powerful legs and its enormous jaws are equipped with several rows of needle-like fangs. Its large, protruding green eyes add the last touch of terror.

As it crept forward it lashed its powerful tail against its yellow sides, and then let out the terrifying roar that often freezes its prey. Its loud voice held no paralyzing terrors for me, and it met cold steel instead of tender flesh. An instant later I withdrew my blade from its heart, and turning toward Tars Tarkas, saw him facing a similar monster. No sooner had he finished his off than I saw another savage creature of the Martian wilds. From then on, for the better part of an hour, one hideous monster after another attacked us, apparently from thin air.

Tars Tarkas was satisfied—here was something that he could cut and slash with his blade. I thought that the diversion was an improvement over the unseen voices. There was nothing supernatural about our new foes. Their howls of pain as they felt our sharp steel in their vitals, and the blood that flowed, was proof enough.

I noticed that the beasts appeared only when our backs were turned; we never saw one materialize from thin air. I knew that the beasts came into the room through some concealed doorways.

Among the ornaments on my friend's leather harness was a small mirror that hung midway between his shoulders on his broad back. Once, as he stood looking down at a newly fallen beast my eyes glanced at this mirror and I saw something that made me whisper, "Do not move, Tars Tarkas! Don't move a muscle!"

He stood like a statue while I watched the wall behind me in his mirror. A portion of the wall was turning, along with a half-round section of the floor directly in front. As it was turning, I could see another beast sitting on the half round floor that had been hidden. When the wall and floor stopped, the beast was facing me on our side of the partition.

But what had interested me most was the sight through the opening. I saw a man who appeared to be operating the controls of the secret doorway. He was neither red, nor green, but white, like myself, with a great mass of flowing yellow hair. There were several red Martian prisoners chained to the wall behind him, along with a number of fierce beasts, ready to be turned loose on us.

As I turned to meet the new beast, my heart was considerably lightened and I whispered, "Watch your end of the chamber! The beasts enter through secret doorways in the wall." I hoped our tormentors did not hear.

As long as each of us remained facing an opposite end of the room, no further attacks were made, so I knew our actions were being observed. Soon a plan of action occurred to me, and backing close to Tars Tarkas I whispered my scheme, keeping my eyes on my end of the room.

The great Thark grunted his agreement, and we slowly moved toward my wall. When we got close enough to the secret doorway we halted back to back. While he remained motionless, I turned my back away from the hidden door so we both faced away from it. I could almost feel eyes watching us.

Quickly my eyes found the mirror and I watched the section of the wall from where the savage monsters had emerged. I did not wait long before the surface started to move. I gave the signal to Tars Tarkas, and jumped through the opening leaving him to fend for himself. A single bound carried me completely through into the adjoining room and brought me face to face with the fellow I had seen before. He was about my own height and well muscled and in every outward detail looked precisely like an Earth man. At his side hung a sword, a dagger, and one of the powerful radium revolvers that are common on Mars.

I was armed only with a sword, and so according to the laws and ethics of battle everywhere on Barsoom, should have been met only with a similar or lesser weapon. This rule had no effect on the moral sense of my enemy, for he whipped out his revolver before I reached the floor by his side! An uppercut from my sword sent it flying from his grasp before he could fire.

Instantly he drew his sword and, now that we were evenly armed, we fought in earnest in one of the closest battles I have ever experienced. The fellow was a marvelous swordsman and obviously trained daily, while I had not gripped the hilt of a sword for ten years before that morning. It did not take me long to rediscover my fighting skills and in a few minutes my opponent realized that he had met his match. He became livid with rage when he realized he could not get through my guard, while blood flowed from a dozen minor wounds on his face and body.

"Who are you, white man?" he hissed. "Your color shows you are no Barsoomian from the outer world! And I know you are not one of us."

But my present business with him did not require any discussion. My present business was to get my sword between his ribs, and in this I was successful within the next few seconds.

The chained prisoners had been watching

our combat in silence; but as my antagonist sank to the floor a cry of warning broke from one of the female prisoners, "Turn! Turn! Behind you!" she shrieked, and as I wheeled around I found myself facing a second man.

This fellow had crept in from a dark corridor and was almost on me before I saw him. Tars Tarkas was nowhere in sight and the secret panel in the wall was closed.

How I wished that he were by my side now! I had fought almost continuously for many hours. I had passed through such experiences and adventures as would sap the vitality of any man, and I had not eaten or slept for nearly twenty-four hours.

I was worn out, and for the first time in years questioned my ability to cope with an opponent. But there was nothing else to do but engage my man. My only plan was to knock him off his feet by the force of my attack—I could not hope to win another long, drawn-out battle.

But the fellow thought differently and he backed and parried and sidestepped until I was almost completely done in. He was a better swordsman than my previous foe, and I could feel myself growing weaker and weaker. Objects started to blur in front of my eyes and I staggered and blundered more asleep than awake.

He backed me around so that I unwittingly stood in front of his dead companion. Then he rushed me so suddenly that I stepped back and fell over the dead man. My head struck the floor with a whack, and to that alone I owe my life, for it cleared my brain and the pain roused my temper! At that moment I was ready to tear him to pieces with my bare hands. I might have tried it except that my right hand came in contact with a bit of cold metal as I struggled on the floor.

The hand of the fighting man has a mind of its own when it comes in contact with a tool of his trade, and I did not need to look to know that the first man's revolver was at my disposal.

The fellow whose trick had put me on the floor was springing toward me, the point of his gleaming blade directed straight at my heart. His cruel and mocking laughter rang out in the room again. And so he died, his thin lips curled in the snarl of his hateful laugh, and a bullet going through his heart.

His body fell on top of me and the hilt of his sword must have struck my head, for I lost consciousness.

CHAPTER 4

Thuvia

It was the sound of conflict that woke me up. For a moment I could not get my bearings. Then, on the other side of the wall, I heard the shuffling of feet, the screams and snarling of beasts, the clank of metal, and heavy breathing. As I rose to my feet, I glanced around the chamber. The prisoners and the savage brutes rested in their chains, eyeing me with expressions of curiosity, rage, surprise, and hope. The latter emotion was on the face of the young red Martian woman whose cry of warning had saved my life.

She was the perfect type of that remarkably beautiful race whose outward appearance is identical with the people of Earth, except that these Martians are of a light reddish copper color. Since she was completely naked, I could not even guess her station in life, though it was evident that she was a slave at the present time.

It was several seconds before the sounds on the opposite side of the wall jolted me back to my senses, and then all of a sudden, I knew that Tars Tarkas was in a desperate struggle. I threw my weight against the secret door, but could not budge it. I looked for a way to open the revolving panel and was about to attack the wall with my sword when the girl called out, "Save your sword, O Mighty Warrior, you will need it more where it will do some good! Do not shatter it against a door which will yield to the lightest touch of one who knows its secret."

"Do you know its secret?" I demanded.

"Yes! Release me and I will get you into the other horror chamber! The key to my lock is on the first of the enemies you killed. But why would you return to face the monsters in that awful trap?"

"Because my friend fights in there alone," I answered as I found the keys.

The fair Martian maid quickly selected the one that opened the lock at her waist, freed herself, and ran to the secret panel. Soon the door swung around along with the floor where I was standing.

The Thark stood in a corner of the room facing a half dozen huge monsters. Their blood-streaked heads and shoulders testified to the swordsmanship of the green warrior. Unfortunately, his glossy hide bore the same mute but eloquent witness to the ferocity of their attacks.

Sharp claws and cruel fangs had torn his legs, arms, and chest to ribbons. He was weak from exertion and blood loss but he still faced his foes—the personification of that ancient proverb of his tribe: "Leave a Thark his head and one hand and he may yet conquer." As he saw me enter, a smile touched his lips, but if it signaled relief, or merely amusement at the sight of my own bloody condition, I do not know.

As I was about to spring into the conflict I felt a gentle hand on my shoulder and found that the girl had followed me into the chamber. She whispered, "Wait, leave them to me," pushed me aside and walked up to the snarling banths.

When she got close to the monsters, she spoke a single Martian word. Like lightning the great beasts wheeled on her, and I thought I'd see her torn to pieces before I could reach her side, but instead the creatures groveled at her feet like puppies. She spoke to them again and started toward the door with the six banths trailing at her heels. She sent them through the doorway and when the last had passed inside we looked at each other in amazement! She turned and smiled at us and then followed them out, leaving us alone.

For a moment neither of us spoke. Then Tars Tarkas said, "She appears to have valuable skills. I heard the fighting on the other side of the partition but I did not fear for you. At least not until

I heard the gun shot! I knew that no man on Barsoom could face you with a sword, but the shot stripped me of my last hope. Tell me what happened."

I related my adventure and, as I finished, the secret panel turned silently and the girl faced us again. She asked, "Who are you? And what is your mission? Why do you attempt escape from the Valley Dor and the death you have chosen?"

"I have not chosen death, maiden," I replied. "I am not of Barsoom, nor have I taken the pilgrimage on the River Iss. My friend here is Jeddak of the Tharks, and though he has not yet expressed a desire to return to the living world, I am taking him with me.

"I am known as John Carter, Prince of the House of Tardos Mors, Jeddak of Helium. Perhaps some rumor of me may have leaked into this hellish place."

She smiled and replied, "Yes, everything that happens in the old world is known here. I have heard of you. The Therns have often wondered where you had gone, since you had not taken the pilgrimage here, nor could you be found on the face of Barsoom."

"Tell me who you are and why are you a prisoner," I asked. "And why do you have power over those ferocious beasts? That skill is far beyond what might be expected of a slave!"

"Yes, I am a slave," she answered. "For fifteen years I've been a slave in this terrible place. And now that they have tired of me I am condemned to die 'the death.'"

"What death?" I asked.

"The Holy Therns eat human flesh, but only that which has died beneath the sucking lips of a plant man—flesh from which the blood of life has been drained. I had been condemned to this cruel death and it was to be within a few hours, but your arrival interrupted their plans."

"Was it Holy Therns who I've been fighting?" I asked.

"Oh, no; those who you killed are lesser Therns, but of the same cruel race. The Holy Therns live on the outer slopes of these hills. They face the broad world from which they harvest their victims.

"Tunnels connect these caves with the palaces of the Holy Therns. The lesser Therns, and hordes of slaves, prisoners, and beasts pass through these tunnels and are the inhabitants of this world.

"Within this vast network of passages and chambers are people and beasts who, born within its dim and gruesome underworld, have never seen the light of day. They are kept here to do the bidding of the race of Therns and to furnish their sport and their sustenance.

"All who reach the Valley Dor are the prey of the plant men and the apes, while their weapons and ornaments are claimed by the Therns. If one escapes the terrible monsters of the valley for even a few hours the Therns claim him. And the Holy Thern on watch, if he sees a victim he desires, takes his prize—this is what happened to me.

"It is said that occasionally some deluded victim of Barsoomian superstition will escape the countless enemies that beset his path and reach the very walls of the Temple of Issus. But what fate awaits him there not even the Holy Therns know, for none who has passed into those gilded walls has ever returned.

"To the Therns, the Temple of Issus is what the Valley Dor is to the peoples of the outer world. It is the ultimate haven of peace, refuge, and happiness to which they pass after this life, and where an eternity is spent amidst the delights of the flesh. This has great appeal to this race of mental giants and moral pygmies."

"I guess the Temple of Issus is a heaven within a heaven," I said. "Let us hope that once there the Therns will reap as they have sown unto others."

"Who knows?" the girl murmured.

"The Therns seem just as mortal as we are, and yet I have always heard them spoken of with the utmost reverence by the people of Barsoom, as one might speak of the gods themselves."

"The Therns are mortal," she replied. "They die from the same causes as you or I. Those who do not die and who live out their one thousand year life span, may go in happiness through the long tunnel that leads to the Temple of Issus."

"We sent several Holy Therns to their death today," said Tars Tarkas, with a laugh.

"And so your death will be all the more terrible when it comes," said the maiden. "And come it will—you cannot escape."

"There was one who escaped centuries ago," I reminded her, "and what has been done before may be done again."

"It is useless even to try," she answered hopelessly.

"But try we will, and you may go with us, if you wish."

"To be put to death by my own people, and my memory made a disgrace to my family and my nation? A Prince of the House of Tardos Mors should know better than to suggest such a thing."

Tars Tarkas listened in silence, but I could feel his eyes on me and I knew that he waited for my answer like one might wait for the reading of his sentence in a court of law.

I replied, "We have the right to escape if we can. Our moral senses will not be offended if we succeed, for we know that the fabled life of love and peace in the Valley Dor is a wicked lie. We know that the valley is not sacred; we know that the Holy Therns are not holy; that they are a race of cruel and heartless mortals, knowing no more than we do of any future life to come.

"Not only is it our right to escape—it is a solemn duty. We should not shrink from this duty even if our own people threaten us with death when we return.

"Only by escape will we carry the truth to those outside, and though they may not trust our story, we should not shirk our duty.

"There is a chance that with several of us testifying our statements may be accepted."

Both the girl and the green warrior stood silent in thought. The girl eventually spoke, "I never considered the matter in that light before. Indeed, I would give my life if I could save a single soul from the torment of this place. Yes, you are right. I will go with you as far as we can go."

I turned an inquiring glance toward the Thark.

"To the mouth of the River Iss, to the bottom of the Sea of Korus, to the snows of the north or to the snows of the south, Tars Tarkas follows where John Carter leads. I have spoken."

"Follow me, now! We could not be further from escape while inside the four walls of this chamber of death."

The girl rotated the secret panel and we stepped into the room with the other prisoners. There were ten red Martians, men and women. Thuvia, the girl who had been so much help, explained our plan and they all decided to join us.

Tars Tarkas and I stripped the bodies of the

two Therns of their weapons, which included swords, daggers, and two revolvers. We distributed the weapons as far as they would go among our followers. With Thuvia holding one of the firearms, she lead us off through a maze of passages, crossing chambers cut out of the solid cliff, following winding corridors, ascending steep inclines, and now and then concealing ourselves in dark recesses at the sound of footsteps.

Thuvia said our destination was a distant storeroom where we might find arms and ammunition. She then would lead us to the top of the cliffs. Once there it would require both intelligence and fighting to force our way through the stronghold of the Holy Therns to the world outside.

"And even then, O Prince," she moaned, "the arm of the Holy Thern is long. It reaches into every nation of Barsoom. Their secret temples are hidden in the heart of every community. If we escape, wherever we go we will find that word of our coming has preceded us. They will try to kill us before we pollute the air with our sinful talk as we tell the truth about this horrible place."

We had proceeded for an hour without interruption. Thuvia had just whispered to me that we were approaching our destination when we came face to face with a Thern.

He was richly dressed but in addition to his leather trappings and jeweled ornaments, he wore a band of gold around his brow. This headband contained a large stone—a duplicate of the one that I had seen on the old man in the atmosphere plant many years before. It is the one priceless jewel of Barsoom.

The stone worn by this Thern was about an inch in diameter. It radiated nine different colors: the seven primary colors of our earthly prism and the two more which are unknown on Earth, but whose wondrous beauty is indescribable.

As the Thern saw us, his eyes narrowed to two nasty slits and he yelled, "Stop! What does this mean, Thuvia?"

For her answer, the girl raised her revolver and fired point blank! Without a sound he sank to the earth, dead, as she hissed, "Beast! After all these years I am avenged at last."

Then she turned toward me and cried, "O Prince, fate is indeed kind to us. The way is still difficult, but through this vile thing on the floor we may yet get to the outer world. Do you see the remarkable resemblance between this Holy Thern and yourself?"

The man was my size and his eyes and features were similar; but his hair was a mass of flowing yellow locks, like those of the two I had killed, while mine is black and close cropped.

"Yes, I see some resemblance, but what about my short, black hair as I try to pose as a yellow-haired priest of this infernal cult?"

She smiled and approached the man she had

just killed. Kneeling down she removed the band of gold from around his forehead, and then, to my amazement, lifted the scalp from the corpse's head! She then placed the yellow wig over my black hair and crowned me with the golden band set with the magnificent gem.

"Now put on his harness, Prince," she said, "and you will pass anywhere you want in the realm of the Therns, for Sator Throg was a Holy Thern of the Tenth Cycle, and mighty among his kind."

As I stooped to the dead man to do her bidding I noted that no hair grew on his head, which was bald as an egg.

"They are all this way from birth," explained Thuvia noting my surprise. "Their original race was crowned with a luxurious growth of golden hair, but for many ages the present race has been entirely bald. The wig has become part of their apparel and they will not appear in public without it."

In another moment I stood garbed like a Holy Thern. At Thuvia's suggestion we carried the dead Thern with us as we continued our journey to the storeroom, which we reached with no problem. Here our stolen keys got us in, and we quickly were outfitted with arms and ammunition.

By this time I was so worn out that I could go no further, so I threw myself on the floor and told some of the released prisoners to keep watch. In an instant I was asleep.

Corridors of Peril

I don't know how long I slept, but I was jarred awake by cries of alarm and a barrage of shots and was on my feet in an instant. A dozen Therns confronted us from the opposite end of the store-room. The bodies of my companions lay around me, mowed down except for Thuvia and Tars Tarkas. They had been asleep next to me on the floor and escaped the attack.

As I got to my feet the Therns lowered their rifles and their faces went pale. I rose to the occasion and demanded, "What is the meaning of this? Is Sator Throg to be murdered by his own servants?"

"Have mercy, O Master of the Tenth Cycle!" cried one of the Therns, while the others edged toward the doorway.

"Ask them about their mission," whispered Thuvia at my elbow.

"What are you doing here?" I demanded.

"Two from the outer world are inside our tunnels. We seek them at the command of the Father of Therns. One was a skilled white fighter, the other a huge green warrior," and here the fellow cast a questioning glance toward Tars Tarkas.

"Here, then, is one of them," spoke Thuvia, indicating the Thark, "and if you will look at this dead man by the door perhaps you will recognize the other. It was left for Sator Throg and his slaves to accomplish what you lesser Therns were unable to do! We have killed one and captured the other. And now in your stupidity you have come and almost killed the mighty Sator Throg!"

The men looked very sheepish and very scared.

"Should they throw these bodies to the plant men and then return to their quarters, O Mighty One?" Thuvia asked me.

"Yes; do as Thuvia says."

As they picked up the bodies, I noticed that one man who helped gather up the late Sator Throg was startled when he looked at the dead man's face. As he helped carry the body from the room, he shot a quick glance at me, and then his eyes fell once more on the bald and shiny dome of the dead man in his arms.

We watched as the last of the gruesome procession disappeared. The girl noticed how skeptical the Thern was and said, "This is not good for us, O Prince, even though that fellow did not accuse us, there are others who will demand a closer scrutiny, and that would prove fatal. Let us flee this place!"

We took off at a fast pace. I was refreshed from my sleep, but still weak from loss of blood and my wounds were painful. No medicinal aid seemed possible. How I longed for the almost miraculous healing power of the salves and lotions of the green Martian women. In an hour they would have had me good as new.

I was discouraged but then the long flowing, yellow locks of the Holy Thern blew across my face. Could this disguise open the way to freedom? If we acted in time, could we escape before the alarm was sounded?

"What will the fellow do first, Thuvia?" I asked. "How long will it be before they return for us?"

"He will go directly to the Father of Therns, old Matai Shang. Matai Shang will not keep him waiting long. If the Father of Therns believes his story we will see searchers everywhere in less than an hour."

"What is the quickest way out of this place?"

"Straight to the top of the cliffs, Prince, and then through the gardens to the inner courts. From there we will go inside the temples of the Therns and across to the outer court. Then the ramparts—O Prince, it is hopeless. Ten thousand warriors could not fight their way out of here!

"Since the beginning of time, little by little, stone by stone, the Therns have been adding to the defenses of their stronghold. A continuous line of fortifications circles the outer slopes of the Mountains of Otz.

"Inside the temples behind the ramparts are a million fighting-men. The courts and gardens are filled with slaves, women and children. No one could go a stone's throw without detection."

"Would we have a better chance after dark?" asked Tars Tarkas. "There seems to be no possibility during the day."

"There would be a little better chance by night, but even then the ramparts are well guarded, though there are fewer outside in the courts and gardens."

"What is the hour?" I asked.

"It was midnight when you released me from my chains," said Thuvia. "Two hours later we reached the storeroom. There you slept for fourteen hours. It must now be nearly sundown again. Come, we will go to a window in the cliff and make sure."

She led the way through winding corridors until we came to an opening with a view of the Valley Dor. At our right the sun was setting, a huge red orb, dropping behind the Otz mountains. A little below us stood the Holy Thern on watch on his balcony. His scarlet robe of office was pulled tightly around him in anticipation of the cold that comes so suddenly with darkness as the sun goes down.

The atmosphere of Mars is so thin that it absorbs little heat from the sun. During the daylight hours it is always extremely hot; at night it is intensely cold. When the great orb of day disappears beneath the horizon, the effect is like extinguishing the only lamp in a room. From brilliant light you are plunged into darkness. Then the moons come; the mysterious, magic moons of Mars, hurtling like monster meteors low across the face of the planet.

The sinking sun lit up the eastern banks of Korus and the gorgeous forest. Beneath the trees we saw many herds of plant men. The adults stood up on their toes with their talons pruning every available leaf and twig. It was then that I understood the careful trimming of the trees that led me to believe that the grove was the playground of a civilized people.

Our eyes wandered to the peaceful River Iss where we saw a canoe carrying a group of red men. They had just emerged from the base of the cliffs on the river.

The eyes of the herald on the balcony spotted the doomed party. He raised his head and voiced the shrill wail that called the demons of this hellish place to the attack. For an instant the brutes stood still, then they poured from the grove toward the river's bank, covering the distance with their long leaps.

The party landed and was standing on the bank as the awful horde came in sight. There was a brief and futile effort of defense. Then silence as the huge, repulsive shapes covered the bodies of their victims and scores of sucking mouths fastened to the flesh of their prey. I turned away in disgust.

"Their part is soon over," said Thuvia. "The great white apes get the flesh when the plant men have drained the blood. Look, they are coming now."

I turned my eyes in the direction the girl indicated and saw a dozen of the white monsters running across the valley toward the river. Then the sun went down and darkness engulfed us and I was spared any more of the frightful scene.

Thuvia lost no time in leading us up through the cliffs toward the surface thousands of feet above. We came upon a few banths wandering loose through the galleries. They blocked our progress but Thuvia spoke a low word of command and the snarling beasts went away.

"If you can fix all of our problems as easily as you control those monsters I can see no difficulties in our way," I said to the girl, smiling. "How do you do it?"

She laughed, and then shuddered and said, "I do not quite know. When I was first brought here I angered Sator Throg when I rejected his advances. He ordered me thrown into one of the banth feeding pits in the inner gardens. Something in my voice, I do not know what, stopped the beasts as they started to attack me.

"Instead of tearing me to pieces, they groveled at my feet. Sator Throg and his friends were so amused by the sight that they kept me alive to train and handle the terrible creatures. There are many of them wandering through these lower regions. They are the scavengers. Many prisoners die here in their chains. The banths solve the problem of sanitation and burial.

"In the gardens and temples above ground they are kept in pits because the Therns fear them. It is because of the banths that the Therns seldom venture below ground except when called by duty."

Thuvia's talent suggested an idea and I asked, "Why not take some banths with us and set them loose on the Therns when we get to the surface?"

Thuvia laughed and said, "I'm sure it would distract their attention from us."

She started calling in a low singsong voice. She continued as we wound our way through the maze of subterranean passages. After a while, soft, padded feet sounded behind us, and I turned and saw a pair of large, green eyes shining in the dark shadows behind. From another tunnel a sinuous form crept toward us. We soon heard low growls and angry snarls on every side as, one by one, the ferocious creatures answered the call of their mistress.

We were surrounded by the brutes! It was a strange experience; the almost noiseless passage of bare human feet and padded paws; the golden walls dotted with precious stones; the dim light cast by the tiny radium bulbs set along the ceiling; the huge beasts of prey crowding around us; the mighty green warrior towering high over the group; me wearing the priceless crown of a Holy Thern; and, leading the procession, the beautiful girl, Thuvia. As we walked I asked her, "Why is it that we see no Therns?"

"They rarely travel in the underworld at night, for that is when the banths prowl the corridors seeking their prey. The Therns fear the inhabitants of this cruel and hopeless world beneath their feet. The prisoners sometimes even rebel and turn on them. A Thern can never tell from what dark shadow an assassin may attack.

"By day it is different. Then the corridors and chambers are filled with guards passing to and fro; slaves from the temples above come by the hundreds to the granaries and storerooms. You did not see the activity because I led you through side passages. But it is possible that we may meet a Thern even now. They do occasionally find it necessary to come here after the sun has set."

But we reached the upper galleries without

detection and Thuvia stopped us at the foot of a short, steep ascent. "Above us," she said, "is a doorway which opens out to the inner gardens. From here all the way to the outer ramparts we will face countless dangers. Guards patrol the courts, temples, and gardens. Every inch of the ramparts is watched by a sentry."

I could not understand the need for such an enormous force of armed men. This spot is so surrounded by mystery and superstition that only the poor souls from the outer world on their last pilgrimage might come near. As we reached a doorway to the outside, I asked Thuvia what enemies the Therns feared.

"They fear the black pirates of Barsoom, O Prince," she said, "may our first ancestors protect us."

The door swung open and the smell of growing things greeted my nostrils and the cool night air blew against my cheek. The banths sniffed the new odors, and then with a rush they broke past us with low growls, swarming across the gardens beneath the light of the nearer moon.

Suddenly a shout came from the roofs of the temples; a cry of alarm and warning that, taken up from point to point, ran off to the east and to the west, from temple, court, and rampart, until it sounded as a dim echo in the distance. The great Thark's sword leaped from its scabbard as Thuvia clung to my side.

CHAPTER
6

The Black Pirates
of Barsoom

"What is it?" I demanded. She pointed to the sky. I looked, and there above us, I saw shadowy aircraft passing back and forth high over the entire realm. Almost immediately flashes of light broke from these flying machines followed by the roar of cannon and then answering flashes and roars came from temple and rampart.

"The black pirates of Barsoom, O Prince!" shouted Thuvia.

The aircraft swept lower toward the defending forces on the ground. Volley after volley were fired on the temple guards; volley on volley flew through the air toward the illusive fliers.

As the pirates swooped closer toward the ground, Thern fighters poured from the temples into the gardens and courts. The sight of them in the open brought a score of fliers darting in to attack.

The Therns fired at them, but on came the air-craft. They were small fliers for the most part, built for two to three men. There were a few larger ones but these kept high aloft dropping bombs on the defenders. With a rush, the pirates dashed reckless-ly to the ground in the midst of the Thern warriors.

Hardly waiting for their craft to touch ground, the creatures leaped among the Therns with the fury of demons. Such fighting! Never had I witnessed its like before. I thought the green Martians were the most ferocious warriors in the universe, but the awful abandon of the black pirates as they threw themselves on their foes went beyond anything I'd ever seen before.

Beneath the brilliant light of the two glorious moons the whole scene was vivid—golden-haired, white-skinned Therns battling hand-to-hand with their ebony-skinned attackers.

Here a little knot of struggling warriors tram-pled a bed of gorgeous flowers; there the curved sword of a black man found the heart of a Thern and left its dead enemy at the foot of a beautiful statue carved from a living ruby; over yonder a dozen Therns attacked a single pirate next to an emerald bench with a strangely beautiful Barsoomian design traced out in inlaid diamonds.

I had heard vague rumors about the black pirates, little more than legends during my for-mer life on Mars. They were thought to inhabit the lesser moon, from where they descended on

Barsoom at varying intervals. When they attacked they committed the most horrible atrocities, and, when they left, carried away loot, firearms and ammunition, and young girls as prisoners. The girls, rumor said, were sacrificed to some terrible god in an orgy that ended with the pirates cannibalizing their victims.

They were large men, over six feet in height. Their features were clear cut and handsome; a slight narrowness of their eyes gave them a crafty appearance. The physical structure of their bodies seemed identical to the Therns and the red men.

I have never witnessed such a lust for blood as these demons displayed in their battle with the Therns. Their flying craft were all around us in the garden and the Therns made no effort to damage the machines. Now and then a black warrior would rush from a nearby temple carrying a young woman in his arms. He would dash straight for his flier while his comrades would cover his escape.

The Therns would attempt to rescue the girl, and in an instant there would be a riot of yelling devils, hacking and stabbing one another. But it always seemed that the black pirates were victorious, and the girl, brought miraculously unharmed through the conflict, was flown away into the outer darkness.

As the fighting receded away from us, Thuvia turned toward me, "Do you understand now, O

Prince, why a million warriors guard the domains of the Holy Therns both day and night?

"The scene you are witnessing now is but a repeat of what I have seen many times during the time I have been a prisoner here. All through history the black pirates of Barsoom have preyed on the Holy Therns.

"Yet they never carry their expeditions to a point where the Therns might be exterminated. They utilize the Therns as playthings while they satisfy their ferocious lust for fighting and collect loot and prisoners."

"Why don't they destroy these aircraft?" I asked. "That would put a stop to the attacks, or at least the blacks would not be so bold. See how they leave their craft with no guards? It's like they were lying safe in their own hangars at home."

"The Therns do not dare attack the flying machines. They tried it once, ages ago, but the next night and for a whole moon thereafter a thousand battleships circled the Mountains of Otz, pouring tons of projectiles down on the temples, the gardens, and the courts, until every Thern who was not killed was driven underground. They were near extermination afterward and they will not risk it again. The Therns know that they live only by the grace of the black men."

Suddenly, a new element was brought into the conflict that surprised both Therns and pirates. Up to now, our banths were frightened by the sound of the battle. But one of them became angered by the noise and excited by the smell of blood, and all at once the large terrifying monster shot into the midst of a struggling mass of humanity. A horrid scream of bestial rage broke from the creature as he felt warm flesh beneath his powerful talons.

His cry was like a signal to the others, and the entire pack hurled themselves among the fighters. Panic reigned—Thern and pirate turned against the common enemy. The awful beasts trampled a hundred men into the ground as they hurled themselves into the thick of the fight. Leaping and clawing, they mowed down the warriors with their powerful paws, turning to rend their victims with frightful fangs.

The scene was fascinating, but suddenly it dawned on me that we were wasting valuable time. We should be using this distraction to get away. The Therns were so engaged with their enemy and the banths that escape might be possible. I searched for an opening through the contending hordes. If we could reach the ramparts we might find a way to the outside world.

As my eyes wandered, the sight of hundreds of aircraft lying unguarded on the ground suggested another way to freedom. I was familiar with every type of flier on Barsoom. For many years I had sailed with the navy of Helium in various ships from a one-man air scout up to the largest battleship in the fleet.

With me, to think is to act. Grabbing Thuvia by the arm, I motioned to Tars Tarkas to follow me and took off. We quickly made it to a small flier away from the battling warriors and jumped onboard. My hands were on the controls and I pressed the repulsion ray button.

The craft swayed slightly but she did not move. Then a yell of warning broke out. I turned and saw a dozen pirates dashing toward us. We had been discovered! On the edge of panic, I continued to press the button that should have sent us racing out into space, but the vessel refused to budge.

Then I realized why she would not rise. We had stumbled onto a two-man flier! Its ray tanks were charged with only enough energy to lift two ordinary men. The Thark's weight was anchoring us to our doom.

The blacks were nearly on us. There was not an instant to lose! I pressed the button, locked it and then set the lever at high speed. As the blacks came up I slipped from the deck and met their attack. The aircraft leaped into the air and I heard Thuvia crying far above my head, "My Prince, O my Prince; I would rather remain and die with—" But the rest was lost in the noise of battle. I knew that my trick had worked and that Thuvia and Tars Tarkas were temporarily safe.

For a moment I thought I'd be overwhelmed. But again, I found that my earthly strength so far overpowered my opponents that the odds were not as bad as they appeared. My blade wove a net of death around me. For an instant the pirates pressed in close with their flashing swords but soon they fell back.

I knew their greater numbers would wear me out and eventually I would go down to certain death. I shuddered at the thought of dying in this terrible place where no word of my death could reach Dejah Thoris.

Then my old-time spirit came back. The fighting blood of my Virginian sires coursed through my veins. The fierce blood lust and the joy of battle surged over me. The fighting smile that has brought fear to a thousand enemies touched my lips. I put the thought of death out of my mind, and charged my antagonists with a fury that those who escaped will remember to their dying day.

I knew that others would press in to support those who faced me, so even as I fought I kept my wits at work, searching for an avenue of escape. It came from an unexpected quarter out of the dark night. I had just disarmed a huge fellow who had given me a desperate struggle, and for a moment the blacks stood back for a breathing spell. They eyed me with fury, yet there was also a touch of respect in their demeanor.

"Thern," said one, "you fight like a Dator. If

not for your detestable yellow hair and your white skin you would be an honor in the ranks of the First Born of Barsoom."

"I am no Thern," I said and just at that moment something hit me between my shoulders and nearly knocked me to the ground.

As I turned to meet this new enemy an object passed over my shoulder, striking one of my assailants squarely in the face and knocking him senseless. At the same instant I saw that it was the trailing anchor of an aircraft floating above us. Instantly I choose this chance for escape. The vessel was slowly rising and the anchor was now several feet above our heads.

With a bound I jumped over the pirates completely. A second leap carried me just high enough to grab the anchor. I hung there by one hand while my astonished enemies yelled beneath me. I was quickly carried beyond the Golden Cliffs and then floated over the Valley Dor and eventually out over the Sea of Korsus, shimmering in the moonlight.

I climbed to a sitting position on the anchor's arms. Then, with the greatest caution, I started to climb up the anchor chain. One hand had just reached the ship's rail when a fierce black face appeared over the side and eyes filled with hate looked into mine.

CHAPTER
7

A Fair Goddess

For an instant the pirate and I remained motionless, glaring into each other's eyes. Then a smile formed on the handsome face as a hand came slowly in sight and the cold, hollow eye of a revolver sought the center of my forehead.

Simultaneously, my free hand shot out for his throat and his finger tightened on the trigger. The pirate's hissing, "Die, cursed Thern," was half choked in his windpipe by my clutching fingers. The hammer fell with a click on an empty chamber. Before he could try again I pulled him so far over the edge that he was forced to drop his firearm and clutch the rail with both hands.

My hold on his throat prevented his outcry, so we struggled in grim silence; he to tear away from my grip, I to drag him over the rail to his death. His face was turning gray and his eyes were bulging from their sockets. He knew he would soon die unless he tore loose from the steel fingers choking the life out of him. He desperately pushed back off the rail and tore at my fingers with both hands.

That was all that I needed. I dragged him completely over the rail and out into space. I did not release my hold on him, however, for I knew that a single shriek as he hurtled to his death would bring his comrades from above.

Instead I held on to him, choking, ever choking, while his frantic struggles dragged me lower and lower toward the end of the chain. Gradually his contortions became spasmodic, lessening until they stopped entirely. Then I released him and in an instant he was swallowed by the shadows below.

Again I climbed to the ship's rail. This time I got my eyes up to the level of the deck, where I could check things out. The nearer moon had passed below the horizon, but the light shining from the farther moon showed the bodies of six or eight sleeping men.

Huddled close to a bench was a young white girl, securely bound. Her eyes had an expression of horrified anticipation and were fixed on me as I climbed onto the deck. They filled with relief as they saw the jewel that sparkled in the center of my stolen headpiece. She did not speak. Instead her eyes warned me to beware of the sleeping figures that surrounded her. The girl nodded to me and I approached her. As I bent low she whispered, "Release me! I can aid you, and you will need all the help you can get when they wake up!"

"Some of them will wake up in the Sea of Korus," I replied smiling.

She caught the meaning of my words, and the cruelty of her answering smile horrified me. One is not shocked by cruelty in some faces, but when it touches the features of a beauty whose face might more fittingly portray love and tenderness, the contrast is appalling.

"Give me a revolver," she whispered. "I can use it on those your sword does not silence."

I found one next to the closest sleeping man and did as she asked. Then I turned toward the distasteful work ahead. This was no time for chivalry that these demons would neither appreciate nor reciprocate. Quietly I went back to the nearest sleeper. When he awoke he was well on his journey to the bosom of Korus. His faint shriek came up to us from the blackness below.

The second one woke up as I touched him, and, though I threw him off the cruiser's deck, his scream brought the remaining pirates to their feet. There were six of them left. As they got up the girl's revolver spoke sharply and one sank to the deck. The others rushed me with drawn swords. The girl did not fire for fear of wounding me, but I saw her sneak to the side and then they were on me.

For a few minutes I experienced some of the hottest fighting I had ever passed through. The quarters were too small for footwork. It was stand your ground and give and take. At first I took considerably more than I gave, but eventually I got beneath one fellow's guard and had the satisfaction of seeing him go down.

The others redoubled their efforts. Sparks flew as steel struck steel, and then there was the dull and sickening sound of a shoulder bone parting beneath the keen edge of my sword. Three now faced me, but the girl was just about to reduce the number by one. Then things happened with such amazing speed that I can barely comprehend what took place.

The three rushed me, forcing me back against the rail. At the same instant the girl fired and my sword arm made two moves. One man dropped with a bullet in his brain; another watched his sword fly clattering across the deck and drop over the edge and the third went down with my blade buried in his chest. As he fell the sword was torn from my hand.

Disarmed myself, I now faced my remaining foe, whose own sword lay somewhere thousands of feet below. The new conditions seemed to please my adversary, for a smile of satisfaction bared his gleaming teeth as he rushed me bare-handed. The muscles coiled beneath his glossy hide probably assured him that here was easy prey, not worth the trouble of drawing the dagger from his harness.

I let him get almost to me. Then I ducked beneath his arms, at the same time sidestepping to the right. Pivoting on my left toe, I swung a terrific right to his jaw, and, like a felled ox, he dropped in his tracks.

A low, silvery laugh rang out behind me. "You are no Thern," said the sweet voice of my companion, "even though you wear golden locks and the harness of Sator Throg. No one has ever lived on all Barsoom who could fight as you have fought this night. Who are you?"

"I am John Carter, Prince of the House of Tardos Mors, Jeddak of Helium," I replied.

She hesitated before speaking, "Are you our enemy?"

"I have been in the territory of the Therns for a day and a half. During that entire time my life has been in constant danger. I have been harassed and persecuted. Armed men and fierce beasts have been set upon me. I had no quarrel with the Therns before, but do you wonder that I feel no great love for them now? I have spoken."

She looked at me intently for several moments before she replied. It was as though she were trying to read my soul, to judge my character and my standards of chivalry in that long, drawn, searching gaze. Apparently the inventory satisfied her. "I am Phaidor, daughter of Matai

Shang, Holy Hekkador of the Holy Therns, Father of Therns, Master of Life and Death upon Barsoom, Brother of Issus, Prince of Life Eternal."

At that moment I noticed that the black I had dropped with my fist was starting to regain consciousness. I sprang to his side, stripped off his harness, and bound his hands behind his back. I then fastened his feet to a heavy gun carriage.

"Why not the simpler way?" asked Phaidor.

"I do not understand. What 'simpler way'?"

With a slight shrug of her lovely shoulders she made a gesture with her hands like the casting of something over the craft's side.

"I am no murderer," I said. "I kill in self-defense only."

She looked at me narrowly. Then she puckered those divine brows of hers, and shook her head. She could not comprehend.

Well, my own Dejah Thoris could not understand my foolish and dangerous policy toward enemies. On the dying planet of Barsoom, quarter is neither asked nor given. Each dead man means more of the planet's waning resources will be divided among those who survive.

But there seemed a difference here between the manner in which this girl contemplated the killing of an enemy and the tenderhearted regret of my own princess for the stern necessity. I think that Phaidor regretted missing the thrill of the spectacle rather than the fact that my decision left another enemy alive.

The man had now regained full possession of his faculties, and was regarding us intently from where he lay tied up on the deck. He was a handsome fellow, clean limbed and powerful, with an intelligent face and such handsome features that Adonis himself might have envied him.

Our vessel had been wandering unguided across the valley; but now I thought it time to take the helm and direct her course. Only in a general way could I guess the location of the Valley Dor. That it was far south of the equator was evident from the constellations, but I was not enough of a Martian astronomer to come much closer than a rough guess. How I missed the splendid charts and delicate instruments I used as an officer in Helium's navy.

I knew a northerly course would lead me toward the more settled portions of the planet. I set the repulsive ray button to send us soaring far up into space. With the speed lever pulled to the last notch, we raced toward the north as we rose above that terrible valley of death.

As we passed over the narrow domains of the Therns, the flash of guns and bombs far below told us that the ferocious battle still raged. No sound reached us at our altitude and it became intensely cold. Breathing was difficult. The girl, Phaidor, and the black pirate kept their eyes glued on me. Finally the girl spoke, "Unconsciousness comes quickly at this altitude, you are inviting death for us all unless you drop quickly."

I followed her advice and not a moment too soon. The girl had fainted along with the pirate, but I retained my senses. We got down to a lower level and were soon traveling above the foothills of the Otz Mountains. It was comparatively warm and there was plenty of air for our starved lungs, so I was not surprised to see the black open his eyes, and a moment later the girl.

"That was a close call," she said.

"It has taught me two things though," I replied.

"What?"

"That even Phaidor, daughter of the Master of Life and Death, is mortal," I said smiling.

"There is immortality only in Issus," she replied. "And Issus is for the race of Therns alone. Thus am I immortal."

I caught a fleeting grin passing across the features of the black as he heard her words. I did not understand why he smiled. Later I was to learn, and she, too, in a most horrible manner.

"The other," I replied, "is that our friend here does not hail from the nearer moon—he passed out, too. If we continued upward much farther he would have died."

Phaidor looked at him in astonishment.

"If you are not from the moon, then where?" she asked.

He shrugged his shoulders but did not reply.

The girl stamped her foot and said, "The daughter of Matai Shang is not accustomed to having her questions unanswered. One of the lesser breed should feel honored that a member of the holy race should even notice him."

Again the black smiled that wicked, knowing smile.

"Xodar, Dator of the First Born of Barsoom, is accustomed to giving commands, not to receiving them," replied the pirate. Then, turning to me, "What are your intentions concerning me?"

"I intend taking you both back to Helium," I said. "No harm will come to you. You will find the red men of Helium a kindly race, but if they listen to me there will be no more voluntary pilgrimages down the River Iss, and the belief they have cherished for ages will be shattered into a thousand pieces."

"Are you of Helium?" he asked.

"I am a Prince of the House of Tardos Mors, Jeddak of Helium," I replied, "but I am not of Barsoom. I am from another world."

Xodar looked at me intently for a few moments and said, "I can believe that you are not of Barsoom, no one of this world could have bested eight of the First Born single-handed. But how is it that you wear the golden hair and the jeweled crown of a Holy Thern?"

I swept the disguise from my head. When the black's eyes fell on my close-cropped black hair they opened in astonishment. "You are indeed of another world," he said, a touch of awe in his voice. "With the skin of a Thern, the black hair of a First Born and the muscles of a dozen Dators it was no disgrace for me to accept your supremacy in battle."

"You are traveling several laps ahead of me, my friend," I interrupted. "I understand that your name is Xodar, but who are the First Born, and what is a Dator, and why, if you were conquered by a Barsoomian, would you not accept it?"

"The First Born of Barsoom," he explained, "are the race of black men of which I am a Dator, or Prince. My race is the oldest on the planet. We trace our lineage directly to the Tree of Life that flourished in the center of the Valley Dor, years ago."

He then launched into a most detailed explanation of the history of Barsoom. He talked of the development of the various life forms such as the plant men, the white apes, the red, green, white, and black men . . . good grief, it seemed like he wanted to talk for hours!

Though I was interested, I wondered why the man took such pains to talk at such length to his enemy. It seemed a strange time for a proud member of a proud race to waste time in casual conversation with his captor.

It was the faintest straying of his eye that explained his motive for dragging out his story. He was in front of where I stood at the controls, so he faced the rear of the vessel as he talked. I caught his eye momentarily fixed on something behind me and then saw the gleam of triumph that brightened those dark orbs. But when I turned to glance behind, the sight I saw froze my hope of freedom.

An immense battleship, cruising silent and unlit through the dark night, loomed close behind us!

CHAPTER 8

The Depths of Omean

Now I realized why the black pirate had kept me engrossed with his story. For miles he had sensed the approach of his rescue, and except for that single glance the battleship would have been directly above us. A boarding party would have swarmed down to our deck, ending my hope of escape. But I was too experienced in aerial warfare to not know how to get out of this mess.

Simultaneously I reversed the engines and dropped my vessel a hundred feet. Above my head I could see the dangling forms of the boarding party as the battleship flew over us. Then I rose at a sharp angle and increased speed. Like a bolt from a crossbow my craft shot its steel prow straight at the whirring propellers of the giant above us. If I could just touch them the huge ship would be disabled for hours and escape might be possible.

At the same instant, the sun rose above the horizon, illuminating a hundred grim faces peering over the stern of the battleship. A shout of rage went up from a hundred throats. Orders were shouted, but it was too late to save the propellers, and with a crash we rammed them.

With the shock of impact I reversed my engine, but my prow was wedged in the hole it made in the battleship's stern! I hung there a second before tearing away, but that second was long enough to have my deck swarming with black devils.

There was no fight. There was no room to fight! We were simply submerged by their numbers. Then, as swords menaced me, a command from Xodar stayed the hands of his warriors, "Secure them, but do them no injury."

Several of the pirates released Xodar. He checked that the girl and I were properly bound and then he had them tie us both together. In the meantime they brought our craft alongside the disabled battleship and we were transported onto her deck. A thousand men crowded around as they tried to get a glimpse of their captives.

The girl's beauty evoked many comments and vulgar jests. It was plain that these pirates lacked refinement and chivalry compared to the red men. My close-cropped black hair and Thern-like complexion were the subjects of much discussion. When Xodar told his fellow officers of my fighting ability and strange origin they asked me many questions.

Without exception the blacks were handsome, well-,built men. The officers were conspicuous through the magnificence of their trappings. Many harnesses were so encrusted with gold, platinum, silver and precious stones that the leather could not be seen.

The harness of the commanding officer was a solid mass of diamonds. Against the ebony background of his skin they blazed. The whole scene was enchanting. The handsome men; the barbaric splendor of their trappings; the polished wood of the deck; the cabins' woodwork inlaid with priceless jewels and precious metals in intricate and beautiful design; the burnished gold of handrails; the shining metal of the guns.

Phaidor and I were taken below decks, where, still tied up, we were locked into a small compartment that contained a single porthole. For some time neither of us spoke. For my part I was wondering about Tars Tarkas and the girl, Thuvia. Even if they eluded pursuit from the pirates they would eventually fall into the hands of either red men or green men. As fugitives from the Valley Dor, they could not look for anything other than a swift and terrible death.

The girl and I were linked together by a rope that allowed us to move only about three feet from each other. I looked toward Phaidor. She was regarding me with a strange expression I had not seen on her face before. She was very beautiful but instantly she averted her eyes, and I thought I saw a delicate flush touching her cheek. I thought she was embarrassed being caught staring at me.

"Do you find the study of the lower orders interesting?" I asked, laughing.

She looked up again with a nervous but relieved little laugh. "Oh very," she said. "Especially when they have such excellent profiles."

I felt that she was poking fun at me, and I admired a brave heart that could look for humor on the road to death, and so I laughed with her.

"Do you know where we are going?" she said.

"To solve the mystery of the hereafter, I imagine."

"I am going to a fate worse than that," she said, with a little shudder.

"What do you mean?"

"I can only guess," she replied, "since no Thern damsel has ever returned to tell of her experiences. The fact they hardly ever take a man prisoner makes me believe that the fate of the girls is worse than death."

"Is it not a just retribution?" I could not help but ask.

"What do you mean?"

"Don't the Therns do the same with the

poor creatures who take the pilgrimage down the River of Mystery? Was not Thuvia a plaything and a slave for fifteen years? Should you not suffer as you have caused others to suffer?"

"You do not understand," she replied. "We Therns are a holy race. It is an honor to be a slave among us. If we did not occasionally save a few of the lower orders that stupidly float down the river, they all would be prey of the plant men and white apes."

"But you encourage the superstition in the outside world!" I argued. "That is the wickedest of your deeds. Can you tell me why you do it?"

She replied, "All life on Barsoom is created to support the Therns. How else could we live if the outer world did not furnish our labor and food? Do you think that a Thern would lower himself to labor?"

"It is true that you eat human flesh?" I asked.

She looked like she pitied my ignorance and said, "Yes, we eat the flesh of the lower orders. Do you not do the same?"

"The flesh of beasts, yes, but not the flesh of man."

"As man eats the flesh of beasts, so may gods eat the flesh of man. The Holy Therns are the gods of Barsoom."

She saw my disgust.

"You are an unbeliever now," she continued gently, "but if we are fortunate enough to escape the pirates and get back to Matai Shang, we could convince you of the error of your ways. And—," she hesitated, "perhaps we could find a way to keep you as—as—one of us."

Again her eyes dropped to the floor, and a faint color came to her cheek. I could not understand her meaning. Dejah Thoris said that in some things I was a simpleton, and I guess she was right.

"I might not return your father's hospitality," I answered. "The first thing I would do if I was a Thern would be to set a guard at the mouth of the River Iss and escort the voyagers back to the outer world. I would also devote my life to the extermination of the plant men and the great white apes."

She looked at me in horror. "No, no," she cried, "you must not say such terrible things—you must not even think them. If they even guess that you entertain such thoughts they would put you to death. Not even my—my—" Again she flushed, and started over. "Not even I could save you."

I said no more. It was useless. She was even more steeped in superstition than the Martians of the outer world.

At this point Xodar opened the door. He smiled pleasantly at me, and said, "Since you cannot escape I do not see the need to keep you confined. You may come up and witness something very interesting. You will see what no one, other than the First Born and their slaves, know about—the entrance to the subterranean Holy Land, to the real heaven of Barsoom.

"It will be an excellent lesson for this daughter of the Therns. She will get to see the Temple of Issus, and perhaps Issus, the goddess, will want to see her."

"What sinful nonsense is this, you dog of a pirate?" she spat. "Issus would wipe out your entire breed before you even came within sight of her temple."

"You have much to learn, Thern, and I do not envy how you will learn it," was his quiet reply.

As we came on deck I saw that the vessel was passing over a vast expanse of snow and ice. I figured we were above the south polar ice cap. Only at the poles of Mars is there ice or snow. No sign of life appeared below.

Xodar was at my side as I stood looking out over the ship's rail. "You will see the Otz Valley soon. We will skirt it for a few hundred miles."

"The Otz Valley! I just escaped from there!" I exclaimed.

"Yes, you crossed this ice field last night before the battleship caught up with us. The Otz Valley lies in a depression at the South Pole. It lies thousands of feet below the level of the surrounding country, like a round bowl. A hundred miles from its northern boundary are the Otz Mountains that form a circle around the inner

Valley Dor. In the exact center of the Valley Dor lies the Lost Sea of Korus. Here you will find the Golden Temple of Issus in the Land of the First Born. That is where we are going."

As I looked I realized why only one man had escaped from the Valley Dor. To cross this frozen, wind-swept waste of ice on foot seemed impossible.

We now reached the southernmost extremity of the great ice barrier. It ended abruptly in a sheer wall thousands of feet deep. At the base of the cliff stretched a level valley, broken here and there by low rolling hills and little clumps of forest, and with tiny rivers formed by the melting of the ice barrier.

Once, we passed far above a deep canyon stretching from the ice wall on the north across the valley as far as the eye could see. "That is the bed of the River Iss," said Xodar.

I soon spotted what appeared to be a flat topped mountain rising from the Sea of Korus.

Xodar was called away to some duty, and Phaidor and I stood alone next to the rail. The girl had not spoken since we had been brought to the deck.

"Is what he has been telling me true?" I asked her.

"In part, yes," she answered. "That about the outer valley is true, but what he says about the location of the Temple of Issus in the center of HIS country is false. If it is not false—" she hesitated. "Oh, it cannot be true, it cannot be true! If it were true then for countless ages my people have gone to torture and death at the hands of their cruel enemies, these black pirates! We believe the location he talked of holds the Temple of Issus where we find the beautiful Life Eternal."

"Just as the lesser Barsoomians of the outer world have been lured by the Therns to the terrible Valley Dor, it seems that the Therns have been lured to an equally horrid fate," I suggested. "It would be an awful payback, Phaidor."

"I cannot believe it," she moaned.

"We shall see," I answered, and then we fell silent again as we watched the rapidly approaching mountain.

As we got close, the vessel's speed slowed until we barely moved. Then we went over the crest of the mountain and below us I saw the mouth of a huge circular well. The diameter of this enormous pit was at least a thousand feet and the bottom was lost in inky blackness.

For a moment the vessel hovered motionless directly above the gaping void, then she slowly began to settle into the black chasm. Lower and lower the monster battleship dropped down into the very bowels of Barsoom.

For half an hour we descended and then the shaft terminated abruptly. We emerged into an immense subterranean world. Above us was the opening of the shaft through the dome-like roof of the incredibly large underground chamber. Below us a vast sea was illuminated by a phosphorescent radiance—the light seemed to come right out of the surface of the rocks. Thousands of ships dotted the ocean. Little islands rose here and there to support the colorless vegetation of this strange world.

Slowly and with majestic grace the battleship dropped until she rested on the water. Her air propellers had been drawn in during our descent and in their place were smaller but more powerful water propellers. The ship took up its journey once more, riding on the water as safely as she had the air. Phaidor and I were dumbfounded. Neither of us had dreamed that such a world existed beneath the surface of Barsoom.

Nearly all the vessels we saw were warcraft. There were a few freighters and barges, but nothing like the number of merchant ships that trade between the cities of the outer world.

"Those ships are the navy of the First Born," said Xodar, watching us with an amused smile.

"This is Omean and that is the Sea of Omean," he continued. "It is larger than the Sea of Korus. It receives the waters of the lesser sea above it. To keep it from filling above a certain level we have pumping stations that force the oversupply back into the reservoirs from where the red men draw the water which irrigates their farm lands."

A new light burst on me with this explanation. Never had the red men been able to fathom the secret source of that enormous volume of water. As ages passed they had simply come to accept it as a matter of course and ceased to question its origin.

We passed several islands with strangely shaped circular buildings. Xodor said they were prisons, watched over by armed guards. Few of these islands contained over an acre of ground, but soon we sighted a much larger island directly ahead. This proved to be our destination, and the ship was soon secured close to the shore.

Xodar signaled us to follow him and we left the battleship and approached a large oval structure.

"You will soon see Issus," Xodar said to Phaidor. "The female prisoners we capture are presented to her. Occasionally she selects slaves to replenish the ranks of her handmaidens. No one serves Issus more than a single year," he added with a grim smile that lent sinister meaning to his simple statement.

Phaidor clung to me, no longer the proud daughter of the Master of Life and Death on Barsoom, but a young and frightened girl in the power of her enemies.

We entered the roofless building. In its center was a long tank of water, set below the level of the floor like a swimming pool. An odd looking craft floated on one side of the pool. As we approached it a hatch opened and a seaman came out.

Xodar addressed him, "Tell your officer that Dator Xodar, escorting two prisoners, must be transported to the gardens of Issus."

"Blessed be the shell of thy first ancestor, most noble Dator," replied the man. "It shall be done." He then saluted and disappeared into the ship. A moment later an officer appeared on deck, welcomed Xodar to the vessel, and we all filed aboard. Phaidor and I were locked in a cabin and almost immediately the vessel began to vibrate.

"Where can we go in such a tiny pool of water?" asked Phaidor.

"From the appearance of the craft I judge we are going down," I replied.

Soon the sensation of sinking became apparent. We could hear the water rushing past the portholes, and in the dim light swirling eddies were visible. Phaidor grasped my arm. "Save me!" she whispered. "Save me and your every wish shall be granted. Anything within the power of the Holy Therns will be yours. Phaidor—" she stumbled a little here, and then in a very low voice, "Phaidor already is yours."

I felt sorry for the poor child, and placed my hand over hers where it rested on my arm. I knew my motive was misunderstood as she wrapped her arms around my neck and pulled my face down to hers.

Issus, Goddess of
Life Eternal

The girl's display of affection touched me deeply but I wondered if she was frightened into it or I had done something to make her believe that I felt the same way. I have never been much of a ladies' man, being more concerned with fighting and similar arts which are more befitting a man than mooning over a scented glove or kissing a dead flower. I had no idea what to do or say.

I'd rather face the wild green hordes of the dead sea bottoms than meet the eyes of this beautiful young girl and tell her what I must tell her. But there was nothing else to be done, and so I did it. Very clumsily too, I fear. I gently took her hands from my neck, and still holding them I told her the story of my love for Dejah Thoris. I told her that of all the women of two worlds that I had known during my long life it was she alone that I loved.

The tale did not seem to please her. Her beautiful face distorted into an expression of hatred and she hissed, "Dog! Dog of the outer world! Do you think that Phaidor, daughter of Matai Shang, begs for your affection? She commands. Your puny outer world passion for the vile creature you chose in your other life is nothing to me!

"Phaidor has glorified you with her love, and you . . . you have spurned her! Ten thousand unthinkably atrocious deaths could not atone for the affront that you have shown me. The thing that you call Dejah Thoris shall die the most horrible death of them all. You have sealed the warrant for her doom.

"And you! You shall be the lowest slave in the service of the goddess you have humiliated. You will be tortured until you grovel at my feet asking for death. In my gracious generosity I will at length grant your prayer, and from the high balcony of the Golden Cliffs I will watch the great white apes tear you to pieces."

She knew the whole lovely program from start to finish. It amazed me to think that one so beautiful could, at the same time, be so vindictive. It occurred to me, however, that she had overlooked one little factor in her revenge. So, without any intent to add to her discomfort, but rather to permit her to rearrange her plans along more practical lines, I pointed to the nearest porthole.

Evidently she had forgotten her present circumstances, for after a single glance at the swirling waters she collapsed on a bench and dissolved into tears. With her face buried in her arms she sobbed more like a very unhappy little girl than a proud and all-powerful goddess.

Finally our downward motion stopped, and I could hear the stern propellers moving us ahead. It was very dark, but the light from our portholes showed that we were forging through a narrow, rock-lined, tunnel. After a few minutes the propellers stopped and we started to rise. Soon the light outside increased and we came to a stop.

Xodar entered and directed us to follow him outside the ship. We found ourselves in a small subterranean vault. As we walked away we saw our submarine in the center of a pool, floating like we had first seen her with only her back showing.

Around the edge of the pool was a level platform. At its edge the walls of the cave rose perpendicularly for a few feet and then arched toward the center of the low roof. The walls around the ledge contained a number of entrances to dim passageways.

Our captors led us through one of the passageways and we entered an elevator. After a rapid ascent we got out and found ourselves in the midst of a veritable fairyland of beauty. The combined languages of Earth could not convey the gorgeous beauty of the scene.

Even I, accustomed to the barbaric splendors of a Martian jeddak's court, was amazed at the glory of the spectacle. Phaidor's eyes were wide in amazement. "The Temple of Issus," she whispered, half to herself.

Xodar watched us with his grim smile of amusement and malicious gloating. The gardens swarmed with brilliantly adorned black men and women. Red and white female slaves moved among them serving their every want. The palaces of the outer world and the temples of the Therns had been robbed of their princesses so that the blacks could have slaves.

We moved through this scene toward the magnificent temple. At the main entrance Xodar spoke a few words to an officer and they entered and remained for some time. When they returned they announced that Issus commanded the presence of both the daughter of Matai Shang and the strange creature from another world who had been a Prince of Helium.

We walked through endless corridors of unthinkable beauty; through opulent apartments and noble halls. After a while we stopped at the doorway to a spacious chamber where we were directed to get down on our hands and knees with our backs toward the room. The doors were swung wide open and after being cautioned not to turn our heads under penalty of instant death we were commanded to back into the presence of Issus.

It was humiliating, and only my love for Dejah Thoris and my hope that I might see her again kept me from rising to face the goddess of the First Born. At least I would have gone down to my death like a gentleman, facing my foes and mingling their blood with mine. After we had crawled in this disgusting fashion almost the entire length of the enormous room our escort halted us.

"Let them rise," said a voice behind us—a thin, wavering voice, yet one that had obviously been accustomed to command for many years.

"Get up," said our escort, "but do not turn toward Issus."

"The woman pleases me," said the thin, wavering voice after a few moments of silence. "She shall serve me the allotted time. The man must go to the prison on the Island of Shador. Let the woman turn and look at Issus, knowing that those who gaze upon her radiant face survive the blinding glory but a single year."

I watched Phaidor from the corner of my eye. She went pale and she slowly, very slowly turned. She was standing quite close to me, so close that her bare arm touched mine as she finally faced the Goddess of Life Eternal. I could not see the girl's face as her eyes rested for the first time on the Supreme Deity of Mars, but I felt the shudder that ran through her trembling flesh.

"Let the woman remain. Remove the man," spoke Issus, and the heavy hand of the officer fell on my shoulder. In accordance with his instructions I dropped to my hands and knees once more and crawled out. It had been my first audience with a deity, but I was not greatly impressed.

Once outside the chamber I was told to rise. Xodar joined me and together we retraced our steps toward the gardens. He said, "You spared my life when you might have taken it. I can help to make your life here more bearable, but your fate is inevitable. You can never hope to return to the outer world."

"What will be my fate?" I asked.

"She often uses men of the lower orders for various amusement. Such a fighter as you, for example, would render fine sport in the monthly Rites of Issus. Men are pitted against both men and beasts for her entertainment and the replenishment of her larder."

"She eats human flesh?" I asked.

"She eats only the flesh of the best bred Holy Therns and red Barsoomians. The flesh of the others goes to our table. Slaves eat the animals."

My reaction to this disgusting concept was ignored as an officer overtook us and said, "Issus wants to look at this man again. The girl has told her that he is of wondrous beauty and of such prowess that he killed seven of the First Born unaided. She also said that he took Xodar captive with his bare hands."

Xodar looked uncomfortable with the thought that Issus had learned of his defeat. Without a word we turned and followed the officer once again to the doors guarding the audience chamber. The ceremony of entrance was repeated. Again Issus told me to rise.

At last the thin wavering voice broke the stillness, repeating in a singsong drone the words that sealed the doom of her victims. "Let the man turn and look at Issus, knowing that those of the lower orders who gaze on the holy vision of her radiant face survive the blinding glory but a single year."

I turned expecting a treat such as only the view of divine glory could produce. What I saw was a solid line of armed men in front of a platform supporting a large throne of carved wood. On this throne sat a very old woman. Not a hair remained on her wrinkled skull. With the exception of two yellow fangs she was toothless. The skin of her face was seamed and creased with a million furrows. Her body was as wrinkled and repulsive as her face. Emaciated arms and legs attached to a torso completed the "holy vision of radiant beauty."

A number of female slaves surrounded her, among them Phaidor, pale and trembling. "Is this the man who slew seven of the First Born and, bare-handed, bound Dator Xodar with his own harness?" asked Issus.

"Yes it is, most glorious vision of divine loveliness," replied the officer who stood at my side.

"Produce Dator Xodar," she commanded. Xodar was brought from the adjoining room. Issus glared at him, a baleful light in her hideous eyes. "And YOU are a Dator of the First Born?" she squealed. "For the disgrace you have brought on the Immortal Race you shall be degraded to a rank below the lowest. No longer are you a Dator, but for evermore you shall be a slave of a slave. Remove his harness. Cowards and slaves wear no trappings."

Xodar stood tall as a guard roughly stripped off his gorgeous trappings.

"Begone!" screamed the old woman. "Begone, you will serve as a slave of this slave who conquered you! You will both go to the prison on the Island of Shador. Take him away out of sight of my divine eyes."

Slowly and with head held high the proud Xodar turned and walked from the chamber. Issus rose and said to me, "You shall be returned to Shador for the present. Later Issus will see how you fight. Go." Then she disappeared, followed by her retinue. Only Phaidor lagged behind, and as I started to follow my guard toward the gardens, the girl came running after me.

"Oh, do not leave me in this terrible place!" she begged. "Forgive the things I said to you, my Prince! I did not mean them. Please take me away with you. Let me share your imprisonment on Shador. We have both looked at Issus and in a year we will die. Let us live that year together in what measure of joy remains for the doomed."

"This is difficult for me, Phaidor, I do not wish to hurt you. I do not want to disrespect the honor you have shown me, but what you desire will not happen. While my heart beats I live for but one woman—Dejah Thoris, Princess of Helium."

Phaidor stood looking at me for a moment. No anger showed in her eyes this time, only a pathetic expression of hopeless sorrow, "I do not understand," she said, and walked slowly away.

The Prison Isle
of Shador

I was escorted to the outer gardens. There I found Xodar surrounded by an angry and taunting crowd. When I appeared they turned their attentions toward me. "Ah," cried one, "so this is the creature who conquered the great Xodar bare-handed. Let us see how it was done!"

"Let him try to fight Thurid," suggested a beautiful woman, laughing. "Thurid is a powerful Dator. Let Thurid show the dog what it means to face a real man!"

"Yes, Thurid! Thurid!" cried a dozen voices.

"Here he is now," said another, and I saw a huge black coming toward us.

"What now?" he cried. "What do you want with me?"

Quickly a dozen voices explained.

Thurid stared toward Xodar, his eyes narrowing to nasty slits.

"Calot!" he hissed. "I always thought you carried the heart of a sorak in your putrid chest. You always beat me in the secret councils of Issus, but now in the field of war your scabby heart has revealed its sores to the world. Calot, I spurn you with my foot," and he turned to kick Xodar.

My blood was up and boiling at the cowardly treatment they had shown this once powerful warrior. I had no love for Xodar, but I cannot stand the sight of something like this.

I was standing close beside Xodar as Thurid swung his foot for the kick. The degraded Dator stood motionless as a statue. But as Thurid's foot swung so did mine, and I landed a painful blow to his shin that saved Xodar from this added insult.

For a moment there was tense silence, then Thurid, with a roar of rage leaped for my throat just like Xodar had done on the cruiser. The results were identical. I ducked beneath his outstretched arms, and as he lunged past me I planted a terrific right punch on the side of his jaw. The big fellow spun, his knees gave way and he crumpled to the ground at my feet. The group gazed in astonishment, first at the still form of the proud Dator lying there in the dust, then at me like they could not believe such a thing could happen.

"You wanted me to treat Thurid the same as I treated Xodor! Now watch!" I then stooped beside the prostrate form, tore off his harness, and tied him securely. "Now do the same to

Thurid as you have done to Xodar. Take him to Issus, bound in his harness, so she sees with her own eyes that there is one among you who is greater than any First Born!

"I am a citizen of two worlds . . . Captain John Carter of Virginia . . . John Carter, Prince of the House of Tardos Mors, Jeddak of Helium! Take this man to your goddess and tell her that I challenge the best of her fighting-men to combat."

Our guard had seen enough and told us it was time to go. We were transported to the Island of Shador where we found a small stone prison and a few blacks stationed there as guards. There was no ceremony wasted in starting our incarceration. One of the blacks opened the door of the prison cell with a huge key, we walked in and the door closed behind us. As the lock clicked, a terrible feeling of hopelessness swept over me.

Last time I was in this kind of fix Tars Tarkas was with me, but now I was alone as far as friendly companionship was concerned. I wondered about the fate of the great Thark, and of his beautiful companion, Thuvia. I knew that even if they escaped and reached a friendly nation, they would never be able to come back here and rescue me.

They could not even guess my whereabouts, for no one on Barsoom even dreamed of this country of Omean hidden beneath the Lost Sea

First Born devils were leaping to the ground all around me.

"They came at me with drawn swords, but before I went down they had tasted the steel of my father's sword. I gave such an account of myself that I know my sire would have been pleased if he'd lived to witness it."

"Your father is dead?" I asked.

"He died before the shell broke to let me into a world that has been very good to me. Except for the sorrow of never knowing my father, I have been very happy. My new sorrow is that my mother must now mourn me as she has mourned my father for the last ten long years."

"Who was your father?" I asked.

He was about to reply when a guard entered and ordered him to his quarters for the night, locking the door after him as he passed through.

"It is the wish of Issus that you two be confined in the same room and that this cowardly slave serve you," he said, indicating Xodar with a wave of his hand. "If he does not, you are to beat him. It is her wish that you heap on him every indignity and degradation you can think of."

With these words he left. Xodar sat with his face buried in his hands. I walked to his side and placed my hand on his shoulder. "Xodar," I said, "you have heard the commands of Issus, but you need not fear anything from me. You are a brave man and it is your own affair if you wish to feel this way, but if I were you I'd assert myself and defy my enemies."

"John Carter, I have been thinking very hard about all the new ideas you gave me a few hours ago. Little by little I have been putting together the things that you said which sounded so sinful to me. I've been comparing them with the things that I have seen in my past life and dared not even think about for fear of bringing down the wrath of the goddess.

"I believe now that she is a fraud; no more divine than you or I. I also am willing to concede that the First Born are no holier than the Holy Therns, and the Holy Therns no more holy than the red men.

"The whole fabric of our religion is based on lies that have been forced on us for ages. Those who wished us to believe these lies did it for personal profit and power.

"I am ready to cast off the ties that bind me. I am ready to defy Issus herself; but what will that do for us? It does not matter if the First Born are gods or mortals, they are still a powerful race, and we are in their clutches. There can be no escape."

"I have escaped from bad spots in the past, my friend, and while life is in me I will try to escape from the Island of Shador and the Sea of Omean."

"But we cannot even escape from the four walls of our prison," moaned Xodar. "Look at this flint-like surface," he cried, slapping the solid rock that confined us. "And look up to the top of this polished wall, no one could scale it."

I smiled and said, "That is the least of our troubles, Xodar. I will scale the wall and take you with me, if you will choose the best time for the escape with your knowledge of the guard routines. Then you must guide me to the shaft that goes up from the dome of this underground sea to the light above."

He quickly replied, "This time of day, after they lock us up for the night, offers the only chance we have, for it is then that the few men on watch are stationed in the tops of the battleships. No watch is kept on the cruisers and smaller craft.

"Even though it is light now do not forget we are far below ground. The light of the sun never penetrates here. The phosphorescent light comes from the rocks that form the dome; it is always bright like this."

"It will make escape more difficult," I said, and then I shrugged my shoulders; for what is the pleasure of doing an easy task?

"Let us sleep on it," said Xodar. "We can think up a plan tomorrow."

So we gave up for the day and slept the sleep of tired men.

When Hell Broke Loose

The next morning Xodar and I started work on our escape plans. First I had him sketch a map of the southern regions. From this I computed the general direction of Helium and its approximate distance. Then I had him draw a map of Omean, indicating the position of Shador and the opening in the dome that led to the outer world.

I studied the maps and talked with Xodar about how the guards patrolled the grounds and performed their other duties. He said that during the evening hours a sentry walked a beat that passed around the prison a hundred feet from the building. The pace of the sentry was very slow, requiring nearly ten minutes to make a circuit. This meant that for nearly five minutes one side of the prison was unguarded.

"This information will be all very valuable AFTER we get out, but how do we escape these walls?" Xodar commented.

"We WILL get out of here," I replied, laughing. "Leave that to me."

"When will we make the attempt?" he asked.

"We go the first night that we know a small craft is moored near the shore."

"But how will you know if any craft is moored nearby? The windows are far beyond our reach."

"Not so, friend Xodar; look!"

With a bound I hopped up fifteen feet, grabbed the bars of the nearest window and took a quick survey of the scene outside. Several small craft and two large battleships were within a hundred yards of the shore. "Tonight," I thought, and was just about to speak when the door of our prison opened and a guard stepped in.

"Where is the white man?" demanded the guard. "Issus commands his presence."

He went into the corridor toward the young red prisoner's cell and I dropped back down beside the astonished Xodar.

"Do you see how we will escape?" I asked him in a whisper.

"I see how you will," he murmured, "but I don't know how I will do it. I certainly can not bounce around like you do."

We heard the guard moving from cell to cell and finally he came back into ours. When he saw me his eyes bulged out from his head.

"By the shell of my first ancestor!" he roared.

"Where have you been? Come with me, Issus commands your presence!"

He took me outside, leaving Xodar behind. There we found several other guards along with the red Martian youth.

The journey back to the Temple of Issus was uneventful. The guards kept the red boy separated from me so we were not able to talk. The youth's face had haunted me. Where had I seen him before? There was something familiar in every line of him; in his carriage, his manner of speaking, even his gestures. I could have sworn that I knew him yet I was sure I had never seen him before.

When we reached the Gardens of Issus we were led away from the temple. Our path wound through beautiful parks to a wall that towered a hundred feet in the air. Massive gates let us out onto a large field surrounded by the same gorgeous forests that I had seen at the foot of the Golden Cliffs. Crowds of First Born were strolling in the same direction that our guards were leading us. Presently we came to our destination, an amphitheatre at the far edge of the plain. The blacks poured in to take their seats while our guards led us under the structure where we found a number of other prisoners.

During the trip from Shador I was not able to talk with my fellow prisoner, but now that we were safely confined I was able to approach the red Martian youth. I asked him, "Are we to fight for the entertainment of the First Born, or is it something worse than that?"

"It is a part of the monthly Rites of Issus in which black men, charged with a crime, wash away their sins in the blood of men from the outer world. If the black is killed, it is evidence of his disloyalty to Issus. If he lives through the contest he is acquitted of all charges brought against him.

"There are different forms of combat. A number of us may be pitted together against a number of blacks; or singly we may be sent out to face wild beasts, or some famous black warrior."

"And if we are victorious," I asked, " . . . freedom?"

He laughed. "Freedom? Forget about it! The only freedom for us is death. No one who enters the domains of the First Born ever leaves. If we prove to be good fighters we are permitted to fight often. If we are not good fighters—" He shrugged his shoulders. "Sooner or later we die in the arena."

"And you have fought often?" I asked.

"Very often," he replied. "It is my only pleasure. Some hundred black devils have I conquered during nearly a year of the Rites of Issus. My mother would be proud if she knew how well I have maintained the traditions of my father's skill."

"Your father must have been a mighty warrior! I have known most of the warriors of Barsoom in my time. Who was he?"

"My father was—"

"Come, calots!" cried the rough voice of a guard. "To the slaughter with you!" and we were hustled into cages looking out into the arena. Unfortunately, I was separated from my youthful friend and he did not occupy a cage with me.

Directly opposite my cage was the throne of Issus. The horrid creature sat surrounded by a hundred slave maidens sparkling in their jeweled splendor. All around her stood heavily armed warriors, elbow to elbow. In front of these guards were the high dignitaries of this mock heaven— decked out in fancy trappings covered with precious stones.

A solid mass of humanity surrounded the throne. The crowd stretched from the amphitheatre's top to bottom and around its entire circumference. There were as many women as men, and each was clothed in the beautiful harness of his rank. With each black was from one to three slaves, captured from the outer world and from the domains of the Therns.

The First Born do not do any labor. The men fight—that is a sacred privilege and duty—to fight and die for Issus. The women do nothing, absolutely nothing. Slaves wash them, slaves dress them and slaves feed them. There are even some who have slaves that talk for them, and I saw one who sat during the rites with closed eyes while a slave narrated to her the events occurring in the arena.

The first event of the day was the Tribute to Issus. It marked the end of those poor unfortunates who had looked upon the divine glory of the goddess a full year before. Ten of them were led into the arena—splendid beauties from the proud courts of mighty jeddaks and from the temples of the Holy Therns. For a year they had served Issus; today they were to pay the price with their lives; tomorrow they would grace the tables of the court.

I watched the gate of a nearby cage thrown open and three monstrous white apes sprang into the arena. The girls backed into a frightened group. One was on her knees with imploring hands stretched toward Issus; but the hideous deity only leaned forward in anticipation of the entertainment to come. At length the apes spied the huddled knot of terror-stricken maidens and with shrieks of frenzy, charged them.

A wave of mad fury surged over me. The blood-red haze that signaled death to my enemies swam before my eyes.

The guard leaned on the unlocked gate of my cage as he watched the show. He thought there was no need for him to keep us poor victims from rushing into the arena of death. A single blow of my fist sent him to the ground out cold. Snatching up his sword, I leaped into the arena. The apes were almost on the maidens, but a couple of bounds were all my earthly muscles needed for me to meet them head on.

For an instant silence reigned in the great amphitheatre, then a wild shout came from the cages of the doomed. My sword circled through the air, and a great ape sprawled, headless, at the feet of the fainting girls.

The other apes now turned on me, and as I stood facing them a sullen roar from the audience answered the wild cheers from the cages. I saw a group of guards rushing toward me from the side. Then a figure broke from one of the cages behind them. It was the red youth!

He paused in front of the prisoner's cages with upraised sword. "Come, men of the outer world!" he shouted. "Let us make our deaths worthwhile and turn this day's tribute to Issus into an orgy of revenge that will echo through the ages! Come! The racks outside your cages are filled with blades!"

Without waiting to see if they would follow, he turned and ran toward me. From every cage that harbored red men a thunderous shout went up in answer to his invitation. The guards went down beneath howling mobs, and the cages spewed out their inmates hot with the lust to kill. They stripped the swords from the storage racks and a swarm of determined armed warriors ran to our support.

The great apes had gone down before my sword while the charging guards were still some distance away. Close behind them pursued the youth. At my back cowered the young girls as I stood there to meet my death. But I knew the land of the First Born would long remember today's events.

I noted the speed of the young red man as he raced after the guards. Never had I seen anything like it in any Martian. His leaps and bounds were little short of those that my earthly muscles could produce. The guards had not yet reached me when he attacked them from the rear, and as they turned, thinking from the fierceness of his onslaught that a dozen men were attacking, I rushed them from my side.

In the rapid fighting that followed I had little chance to note anything other than the movements of my immediate adversaries. But now and then I caught a glimpse of a swinging sword and a figure of powerful action that filled my heart with a strange yearning and an unaccountable pride. A grim smile was on the boy's handsome face and he always seemed to throw a taunting challenge to the foes that faced him. In this and other ways his manner of fighting was similar to mine. Perhaps it was this likeness that made me love the boy, while the havoc that his sword played among the enemy filled my soul with respect.

The two of us were having a merry time of it when a large body of the goddess's guards charged into the arena. They came at us with fierce cries, while from every side the armed prisoners swarmed into them. For half an hour it was as though all hell had broken loose. In the walled confines of the arena we fought in a swarming mass—howling, cursing, blood-streaked demons—and always the sword of the young red fighter flashed beside me.

I formed the prisoners into a rough formation, so that we fought in a circle around the doomed maidens. Many had gone down on both sides, but by far the greater havoc had been done to the guards. I could see messengers running up into the stands and as they passed through the audience the nobles unsheathed their swords and ran down into the arena. It was plain they were going to annihilate us by their shear force of numbers.

I caught a glimpse of Issus on her throne, her hideous face distorted in a horrid grimace of hate and rage and fear. Quickly I ordered fifty of the prisoners to drop back behind us and form a new circle around the maidens. "Remain and protect them until I return!" I shouted.

Then, turning to those who formed the outer line, I yelled, "Down with Issus! Follow me to the throne! We will reap vengeance where vengeance is deserved!"

The youth at my side was the first to take up the cry of "Down with Issus!" and then at my back and from all sides came a hoarse shout, "To the throne! To the throne!"

As one irresistible fighting mass we moved over the bodies of dead and dying foes toward the throne of the Martian deity. Hordes of First Born fighting-men poured out from the audience to stop our progress. We mowed them down like they were made of paper.

"To the seats, some of you!" I cried as we approached the arena's barrier wall. "Ten of us can take the throne," for I had seen that most of her guards had entered the fight in the arena. The prisoners broke to left and right for the seats, vaulting the low wall with swords lusting for the victims in the crowd. In another moment the entire amphitheatre was filled with the shrieks of the dying and wounded, mingled with the clash of arms and triumphant shouts of the victors.

Side by side the young red man and I, with just a few other fighters, hacked our way to the foot of the throne. The remaining guards, reinforced by the high dignitaries and nobles of the First Born, closed in to protect Issus, who sat leaning forward on her carved bench, screaming and cursing those who sought to desecrate her godhood.

The frightened slaves around her trembled, not knowing whether to pray for our victory or for our defeat. Several of them, proud daughters of some of Barsoom's noblest warriors, snatched swords from the hands of the fallen and fell on the guards, but they were soon cut down; beautiful martyrs to a hopeless cause.

Never since Tars Tarkas and I fought out that long, hot afternoon against the hordes of Warhoon, had I seen two men fight to such good purpose and with such ferocity as the young red man and I fought that day. Man by man those who stood between us and the throne went down before our blades. Others swarmed in to fill the breach, but foot by foot we got nearer to our goal.

Suddenly a cry went up from a section of the stands near by—"Rise slaves! Rise slaves!" It swelled to a mighty volume of sound that swept around the entire amphitheatre.

For an instant we ceased our fighting to look for the meaning of this new outburst. In all parts of the structure the female slaves were attacking their masters with any weapon they could find. A dagger snatched from the harness of her mistress was waved aloft by some fair slave, its shimmering blade crimson with the lifeblood of its previous owner; swords plucked from the bodies of the dead; heavy ornaments which could be turned into bludgeons—such were the implements these fair women used to wreak their vengeance on their masters. It was a sight to make one cheer; but in a brief second we were engaged once more in our own contests with only the battle cry of the girls to remind us that they were still fighting— "Rise slaves! Rise slaves!"

Only a single rank of men now stood in front of Issus. Her face was blue with terror. Foam flecked her lips. She seemed paralyzed with fear. Only the youth and I fought now. The others had fallen, and I was almost struck down—but a hand reached out from behind my adversary and grabbed his elbow as his blade was falling. The youth rushed to my side and ran his sword through the fellow before he could recover to deliver another blow. As the man fell I looked behind him into the eyes of the one whose quick hand had saved me—it was Phaidor, daughter of Matai Shang.

"Fly, my Prince!" she cried. "It is useless to fight them any longer. Everyone down in the arena is dead. All of the slaves who charged the throne are dead except for you and this youth. Only a few of your fighting men are left among the seats, and they are fast being cut down. You can scarcely hear the battle cry of the slave girls for nearly all of them are dead. Break for the open and the Sea of Korus. With your strong sword arm you may get to the Golden Cliffs and the gardens of the Holy Therns. When you get there tell your story to my father, Matai Shang. He will make you one of his officers, and together you may find a way to rescue me. Fly while you have a chance!"

But that was not my mission, and I could not see much to be preferred between the cruel hospitality of the Holy Therns compared to that of the First Born. "Down with Issus!" I shouted, and together the boy and I took up the fight once more. Two blacks went down with our swords in their vitals, and we stood face to face with the goddess. As my sword went up to end her horrid career she turned to flee with an ear-piercing shriek. The flooring of the throne's platform fell away behind her revealing a dark tunnel. She sprang for the opening with the two of us close at her heels. Her scattered guard rallied at her cry and rushed for us. A blow staggered the youth, but I caught him in my left arm and turned to face the infuriated mob.

Doomed to Die

For an instant I stood my ground, but their charge forced me back a step. My foot felt for the floor but found only empty space. I had backed into the pit that had just swallowed Issus! For a second I toppled there on the brink then I, with the boy still tightly clutched in my arm, pitched backward into the black abyss.

We were sliding down some kind of polished chute, the opening above us closed as magically as it had opened, and we shot down into a dim chamber far below the arena. As I rose to my feet the first thing I saw was Issus glaring at me through the heavy bars of the only door out of the room.

"Rash mortal!" she shrieked. "Here, in this secret cell, you shall pay the penalty for your sinful talk against me! Here you shall lie alone and in darkness with the carcass of your accomplice festering by your side! You will stay here until,

121

crazed by loneliness and hunger, you feed on the crawling maggots that were once your comrade."

In another instant she was gone, and the cell's dim light faded into blackness.

"Pleasant old lady," said the voice of the youth.

"Thank God you are not dead," I said. "That was a nasty cut on your head."

"It just stunned me," he replied. "A mere scratch."

"We seem to be in a pretty fix here with a good chance of dying of starvation and thirst."

"Where are we?"

"Beneath the arena. We tumbled down the shaft that swallowed Issus as she was almost at our mercy."

He laughed a low laugh of pleasure and relief, and then whispered, "Nothing could be better. There are secrets here in the palace of Issus that the goddess herself could not even dream of."

"What do you mean?"

"I worked here with other slaves in the remodeling of these subterranean galleries, and we found an ancient system of corridors and chambers that had been sealed up for ages. I know the entire system perfectly.

"There are miles of corridors honeycombing the ground beneath the gardens and the temple, and there is one passage that leads down to the lower regions that open onto the water passage to the Sea of Omean.

"If we can reach the submarine undetected we can make it to the sea. There we can find many islands where the blacks never go. We could live safely for some time, and who knows what else could happen to aid us in our escape!"

He had spoken in a low whisper, fearing spying ears, and so I answered him in the same subdued tone, "Lead back to Shador. My friend, Xodar, the black, is there. We were planning to escape together, so I cannot desert him."

"I agree," said the boy, "one cannot desert a friend. It would almost be better to get recaptured than to do that."

I heard him searching the floor of the dark room. After a few minutes he quietly called me and I crept toward the sound of his voice. Feeling around in the dark I finally found him kneeling on the brink of a trap door opening in the floor.

"There is a drop here of about ten feet," he whispered. "Hang by your hands and you will land safely on a level floor of soft sand."

Very quietly I lowered myself from the pitch black cell into the inky pit below. It was so dark that I could not see my hand in front of my face. For an instant I hung in mid air. When the distance below is shrouded in darkness there is a feeling like panic at the thought of taking the plunge into an unknown depth. Then I released my hold and dropped—four feet to a cushion of sand. The boy followed me.

"Raise me to your shoulders and I will replace the trap door," he said quietly.

This done he led me very slowly down a very steep incline. "It will not be long before we have light. At the lower levels we meet the same strata of phosphorescent rock that illuminates Omean."

After a short time there was a low exclamation from the boy, "At last, the lighted way!"

As I looked up the tunnel I saw a dim radiance. The light increased and from then on our progress was rapid until we came to the end of a corridor that let directly onto the ledge surrounding the pool of the submarine.

The craft lay at her moorings with her hatch open. Raising his finger to his lips and then tapping his sword in a significant manner, the youth crept noiselessly toward the vessel. I was close at his heels.

Silently we climbed onto the deserted deck and crawled to the hatchway. A glance below revealed no guard in sight, and so we quietly dropped into the submarine. There was no sign of life. Quickly we secured the hatch.

The boy touched a button and the boat quickly sank amid swirling waters. Even then there was no scurrying of feet as we had expected, and while the boy remained to control the boat I went from cabin to cabin in search of the crew. I found the craft was completely deserted. Such good fortune seemed almost unbelievable. When I returned to report the good news to my companion he handed me a paper and said, "This may explain the absence of the crew."

It was a radio message to the commander of the submarine: "The slaves have risen. Come with what men you have and those that you can gather on the way. The slaves are massacring everyone in the amphitheatre. Issus is threatened. Make haste, ZITHAD."

"Zithad is Dator of the guards of Issus," explained the youth. "We gave them a bad scare—one that they will not soon forget."

We reached the submarine pool in Omean without incident. Here we debated the wisdom of sinking the craft but finally decided that it would add nothing to our chances for escape. We were now in a quandary as to how to get past the guards who patrolled the island. At last I thought of a plan.

"What is the name of the officer in charge of these guards?" I asked the boy.

"A fellow named Torith was on duty this morning," he replied.

"Good. And what is the name of the commander of the submarine?"

"Yersted."

I found a blank dispatch form in the cabin and wrote the following order: "Dator Torith: return these two slaves at once to Shador. "YERSTED."

I handed the forged order to the boy. "Come, we shall see how well it works."

"But our swords!" he exclaimed. "What will we say to explain them?"

"Since we cannot explain them we'll have to leave them behind," I replied.

"But should we put ourselves in the power of the First Born again without weapons?"

"It is the only way," I answered. "You must trust me to find a way out of the prison, and I know that once we get out, we will not have any difficulty finding weapons in this place which contains so many armed men."

"As you say," he replied with a smile and shrug. "Let us put your plan to the test."

We emerged from the sub's hatchway and strode over to the sentry's post. The guardsmen sprang up in surprise, and demanded we stop. I held out the fake message to one of them. He took it and handed it to Torith as he emerged from his office. The officer read the order, and eyed us with suspicion. "Where is Dator Yersted?" he asked.

I cursed myself for not having sunk the sub-marine to cover my next lie, "his orders were to return to the temple's submarine landing."

Torith took a half step toward the pool as though to corroborate my story. At that instant everything hung in the balance, if he went over and found the empty submarine the whole fabric of my concoction would be exposed. But he decided the message was genuine—there was no reason to doubt it since it would be unbelievable for two slaves to put themselves into custody like this. It was the very boldness of the plan that made it successful.

"Were you connected with the rising of the slaves?" asked Torith. "We have received reports of some such event."

"All the slaves were involved," I replied. "But it amounted to little. The guards quickly killed the ringleaders."

He seemed satisfied with this reply. "Take them to Shador," he ordered, and in a few minutes we were on the island. Here we were returned to our respective cells; I with Xodar, the boy by himself. And so we were again prisoners of the First Born.

A Break for Liberty

Xodar was astonished as I told him of the events at the Rites of Issus. Though he had already expressed his doubt about the supposed goddess, he could hardly conceive that we could threaten her with sword in hand and not be blasted into fragments by her divine power.

"It is the final proof," he said at last. "No need to say any more to shatter the last remnant of my belief in the goddess. She is only a wicked old woman who wields her power for evil. She has kept her own people and all Barsoom in religious ignorance for ages."

"She is still all-powerful here, however. So it is best for us to leave as quickly as we can," was my reply.

"It will soon be night," said Xodar. "How may I aid in the adventure?"

"Can you swim?" I asked him.

"No slimy eel that haunts the depths of Korus is more at home in water than I am!" he boasted.

"Good. The red one cannot swim and I want to take him with us. Even the bravest of the red men are terrorized at the mere thought of deep water, for it has been ages since their ancestors saw a lake, river, or sea. One of us will have to support him in the water as we swim to our escape craft."

Xodar nodded his head in agreement and said "The boy's sword will be welcome. I have seen him battle at the Rites of Issus many times. Until I saw you fight, I had never seen anyone else who seemed so unbeatable. One might think you two were master and pupil, or father and son. There is a resemblance between you. It is very marked when you fight—there is the same grim smile and the same maddening contempt for your adversary."

"Yes, I witnessed his skills today and he is a great fighter. I think that we will make a trio difficult to beat, and if my friend Tars Tarkas the Thark were with us we could fight our way from one end of Barsoom to the other."

"We may have to fight from one end of Barsoom to the other when they find out we have come back from the Valley Dor. That is one of the many edicts Issus has fostered on Barsoom. She works through the Holy Therns. Her decrees are mysteriously delivered to their heavily guarded altars. They think no one could gain access into their innermost alter chambers. I myself have delivered these messages by way of a secret tunnel to the temple of Matai Shang.

"The Therns have temples located around the entire civilized world. Their priests communicate the doctrines of Issus to the people. They persuade the poor deluded creatures to take the pilgrimages that swell the wealth of the Holy Therns and add to the numbers of their slaves.

"The Therns collect the wealth and labor from all Barsoom and then the First Born take it from the Therns. Occasionally the First Born make raids on the outer world, as well. It is then that they capture females from the royal houses of the red men. They also steal weapons and fighting ships and even kidnap the trained engineers and mechanics who build them.

"We are a non-productive race and we are proud that we do no work. It is criminal for a First Born to do any labor. That is for the other races who only live so that the First Born may enjoy long lives of luxury and idleness. With us, fighting is all that counts. If it were not for fighting there would be more of the First Born than all the creatures of Barsoom could support, for none of us ever dies a natural death."

Suddenly, the signal marking the end of the day rang out. It was time for the men of Omean to spread their silks and fall into the dreamless sleep of Mars. I waited a few minutes and then jumped up to the window and surveyed the nearby waters. Just off the island, a quarter of a mile perhaps, was a monster battleship. Between her and the shore were a number of smaller cruisers and one-man scouts. I spotted only one sentry— I could see him plainly in the upper works of the battleship—and as I watched I saw him bed down for the night. The discipline on Omean was lax indeed. I dropped to the floor and described the various craft I had seen with Xodar.

His eyes lit up as he said, "My personal craft is still out there! It is built to carry five men and is very fast. If we can get to her we will have our best chance to escape," and then he went on to describe the equipment on the craft; her engines, and all the components that went to make her one of the fastest fliers in the fleet.

We decided to wait for the guards to settle down and in the meantime I would bring the red youth to our cell. I jumped up to the top of our partition wall to find a flat surface about a foot wide. I walked along this until I came to the cell where I saw the boy sitting on his bench. He had been leaning back against the wall looking up at the glowing dome above Omean, and when he saw me on the partition wall above him his eyes opened wide in astonishment.

As I stooped to drop to the floor beside him he motioned me to wait and whispered: "Catch my hand; I can almost leap to the top of that wall myself. I have tried it many times, and each day I get a little closer. Someday soon I would have made it."

I lay down on the ledge and reached my hand down. With a little run he jumped up and I caught his outstretched hand and then pulled him up beside me. We returned to my cell and finalized our escape plans with Xodar. We knew that even if we escaped the First Born we would still have a whole world against us—religious superstition is a powerful force.

With a final glance around our prison I said, "Now is as good a time as any. Let's go."

Another moment found me at the top of the cell wall with the boy beside me. I unbuckled a long strap from my harness and lowered it to Xodar. He grabbed the end and was soon sitting beside us.

"How simple," he laughed.

"I hope the rest is as simple," I said and then I raised myself to the top of the outer wall to locate the passing sentry. I waited a few minutes and he came in sight on his slow walk around the structure.

I watched him until he had made the turn at the end of the building. The moment he disappeared I used my harness strap to lower Xodar to the ground. Then the boy used the strap to slide down beside Xodar.

According to our plan, they did not wait for me, but took off immediately for the water, sneaking past the guardhouse with its sleeping soldiers. I dropped to the ground and followed them but as I passed the guardhouse the thought of all the good weapons inside made me pause. I glanced at Xodar and the youth and saw that they had slipped over the edge of the dock into the water and were already making their way toward our escape craft.

The lure of the swords inside the structure was strong and I hesitated, but another moment saw me creeping toward the door. I pressed it open just enough to see a dozen blacks stretched out on their silks fast asleep. At the far side of the room was a rack filled with swords and firearms. One of the men stirred, and my heart stood still. I worried about jeopardizing our escape; but decided to see the adventure through.

With a spring as noiseless as a cat's I landed beside the guardsman who had moved. My hands hovered over his throat waiting for his eyes to open. I stayed like that for what seemed an eternity but finally the fellow turned on his side and resumed the even breathing of deep slumber.

I picked my way between and over the soldiers until I was at the rack. I turned to survey the sleeping men. All were quiet. Their regular breathing rose and fell in a soothing rhythm that seemed like the sweetest music I had ever heard.

Gingerly I drew a sword from the rack. As I removed it, the scraping of its scabbard sounded like the filing of cast iron with a rasp, and I expected to see the room immediately filled with attacking guardsmen. But no one stirred.

The second sword I got out noiselessly, but the third clanked in its scabbard with a frightful din. I knew that it must have disturbed at least some of the men, and was about to run for the doorway, when again, to my surprise, not a man moved.

I was about to leave when the revolvers caught my eye. I knew that I could not carry more than one, for I was already too loaded down to move quietly. As I took one from its pin my eye fell for the first time on an open window beside the rack. Ah, here was a splendid means of escape, for it led out onto the dock, right at the water's edge.

As I congratulated myself, I heard the door open, and there, looking me straight in the eye, stood the officer of the guard! He took in the situation at a glance and appreciated the gravity of it as quickly as I did, for our revolvers came up at the same time and the two shots sounded simultaneously.

I heard his bullet as it whizzed past my ear, and at the same instant saw him crumple to the ground. Where I hit him I do not know, for scarcely had he started to collapse when I was through the window. In another second I was in the water swimming to the flier following my partners.

Xodar was burdened with the boy and I with the three swords. I had dropped the revolver. While we were both strong swimmers it seemed to me that we moved at a snail's pace. I was swimming underwater, but Xodar had to rise often to let the youth breathe, so it was a miracle we reached the boat. We were all aboard before the watch on the battleship saw us. Then an alarm gun bellowed, its deep boom reverberating beneath the rocky dome of Omean. Instantly the sleeping thousands were awake and the decks of every warcraft swarmed with fighting-men.

We cast away before the sound of the first gun died, and another second saw us rising swiftly from the surface of the sea. I was at the controls with Xodar and the boy stretched prone behind me, to offer as little air resistance as possible.

"Climb high!" yelled Xodar. "They won't fire their heavy guns toward the dome—shell fragments might drop back among their own craft. If we are high enough our keel plates will protect us from small-arms fire."

"A little to your right," he cried. There are no points of the compass in Omean where every direction is due north. The pandemonium that had broken out below us was deafening. Rifles cracked, officers bellowed orders, men yelled directions to one another from the shore and from the decks of boats, while the sound of countless propellers cutting water and air was overpowering.

I dared not pull my speed lever to the highest for fear of overrunning the mouth of the shaft that passed up through Omean's dome to the world above, but even so we were racing along.

The smaller fliers were starting to rise toward us when Xodar shouted: "The shaft! The shaft! Dead ahead," and I saw the opening, black and yawning in the glowing dome of this hellish underworld.

A ten-man cruiser was rising directly in front of us to cut off our escape. It was the only vessel near by, but at the rate that it was moving it would block our path. It was climbing at a steep angle, ready to snag us with grappling hooks as it skimmed over our deck.

There were very few options. It was no good to climb higher; that would have allowed her to force us against the rocky dome. If I tried to dive below it would put us precisely where she wanted us. On either side a hundred other menacing craft were charging toward us.

As we approached the cruiser, I steered our flier so she looked as if we were trying to gain altitude on the enemy ship. The cruiser attempted to climb at a steeper angle to block our path. Then, right before we might have passed over the larger ship, I yelled to my companions to hold tight, set the throttle lever to its highest speed, and aimed straight for the cruiser's keel.

Her commander may have seen my intentions but it was too late. Almost at the instant of impact I turned my bows upward, and then with a shattering jolt we collided. The cruiser, already tilted up at a dangerous angle, was carried completely over backward by the impact. Her crew fell twisting and screaming down to the water far below, while the cruiser, her propellers still churning, followed.

The collision crushed our bow and almost threw us off the deck. We landed in a wildly clutching heap at the very edge of the flier. Xodar and I grabbed the handrail, but the boy would have gone overboard if I had not snatched his ankle.

Unguided, our vessel careened wildly, rising dangerously toward the rocks above. It took but an instant for me to regain control, and with the roof barely fifty feet above I turned her nose once more toward the black mouth of the shaft.

The collision had slowed our progress and now a hundred swift scouts were closing in on us. Xodar had told me previously that going up the shaft slowly by using our repulsive rays alone would give our enemies their best chance to overtake us, since our propellers would be idle.

There were now so many boats around us it looked like we would be quickly caught in the shaft. To me there always seems a way to gain the opposite side of an obstacle. If one cannot pass over it, or below it, or around it, there is but a single alternative left, and that is to pass through it.

"Reverse!" screamed Xodar. "For the love of your first ancestor, reverse! We are at the shaft!"

"Hold tight!" I ordered in reply. "Grab the boy and hold tight—we are going straight up the shaft!"

The words were barely out of my mouth as we swept beneath the pitch-black opening. I pointed the bow straight up, pushed the speed lever to its fastest setting again and, clutching a guard rail with one hand and the steering wheel with the other, hung on. I heard an exclamation of surprise from Xodar, followed by a grim laugh. The boy laughed too and said something I could not catch because of the whistling wind.

I looked above my head, hoping to catch the gleam of stars so I could steer the ship through the center of the tunnel. If we touched the side at this speed it would be instant death for us all. But not a star showed above—only impenetrable darkness.

Then I glanced below and saw a rapidly diminishing circle of light—the mouth of the opening above the phosphorescent radiance of Omean. I steered by this, trying to keep the circle of light centered below. We were not in the shaft very long, Omean lies perhaps two miles below the surface. At two hundred miles an hour, we were in the shaft less than forty seconds.

We were out before I knew it! But darkness was all around us. There were neither moons nor stars. I had never before seen such a thing on Mars with her crystal clear skies. Then the explanation came to me. It was summer at the South Pole. The ice cap was melting and clouds and fog—unknown on the large desert part of Barsoom—were shutting out the nighttime light of heaven. We escaped through nature's curtain that hid us from our pursuing enemies.

We went through the cold damp fog without slowing down and soon emerged into the glorious light of the two moons and a million stars. I dropped lower and headed due north. Our enemies were a good half-hour behind us. We had performed the miraculous and come through a thousand dangers unscathed—we had escaped from the land of the First Born!

As Xodar and I glanced at each other in relief, he said, "No one else could have done this but John Carter."

At the sound of my name the boy jumped to his feet.

"John Carter!" he cried. "John Carter! Why, John Carter, Prince of Helium, has been dead for years! I am his son!"

The Eyes in the Dark

My son! I could not believe my ears! Slowly I rose and faced the handsome youth. Now that I looked at him closely I saw why his face and personality had affected me so strongly. There was much of his mother's beauty in his clear-cut features, but it was strongly masculine beauty, and his gray eyes were mine.

The boy stood facing me with a look of half hope and half uncertainty.

"Tell me about your mother," I said. "Tell me all you can of the years that I have been robbed of being with her."

With a cry of pleasure he came to me and threw his arms around my neck, and tears welled in my eyes as I held him close. I almost choked like some emotional fool—but I do not regret it, nor am I ashamed. A long life has taught me that a man may seem weak where women and children are concerned and yet be anything but weak in the sterner avenues of life.

"Your stature, your manner, your swordsmanship," said the boy, "are just like my mother described them a thousand times! But, do you know what convinced me most?"

"What, my boy?"

"Your first words to me—you asked about my mother. No one but the man who loved her like my father would have thought of her first."

"For many long years, my son, I can hardly recall a moment that your mother has not been on my mind. Tell me about her."

"Those who have known her longest say that she has not changed, unless it was to grow more beautiful—if that were possible. Sometimes, though, when she thinks I'm not watching, her face grows very sad, and, oh, so wistful. She always thinks of you, my father, and all Helium mourns with her and for her. Her grandfather's people love her. They also love you, and worship your memory as the savior of Barsoom.

"Each year on the anniversary of the day you saved Barsoom a giant festival is held in your honor; but there are tears mingled with the thanksgiving—tears of regret that you are not with us to share the joy. There is no greater name than John Carter on all Barsoom."

"And by what name has your mother called you, my boy?" I asked.

"The people of Helium asked that I be named after my father, but my mother said no, that you and she had already chosen a name. She said your wish must be honored, so my name is the one you wanted—Carthoris—a combination of hers and yours."

Xodar had been at the wheel as I talked with my son, but I noticed he was having trouble controlling the ship. He turned and said, "She is dropping badly at the bow! As long as we were rising at an angle it was not noticeable, but now that I am trying to keep a level course it is different. The collision damage has opened one of her ray tanks!"

After we examined the damage it was worse than we thought. Not only were we slowing down, but at the rate that we were losing our repulsive rays we would soon sink to the ground.

I took the helm and set the engine wide open. In the meantime Carthoris and Xodar were puttering with the damaged bow in a hopeless attempt to slow down the escaping rays.

It was still dark when we passed the boundary of the ice fields. Below us lay a typical Martian landscape. Rolling depressions of long dead seas with their surrounding hills, and here and there the grim and silent cities of the past. These were now inhabited only by age-old memories of a once powerful race, and by the great white apes of Barsoom.

It was becoming more and more difficult to keep our little vessel in the air. The bow sagged lower and lower until we had to stop the engine to prevent our flight terminating in a swift dive down to the ground.

As the sun rose our craft gave a spasmodic lurch, turned half on her side, and then went in a slow circle, her bow dropping further each moment. We held on to the handrails, and since I was close to the controls, I reached out to the repulsion ray lever. The boat responded to the touch, and very gently we began to sink.

A short while later we were on the ground surrounded by the beautiful flowering plants that grow in the arid places of Barsoom. We found many of the huge milk-giving shrubs—the strange plant which serves as food and drink for the wild hordes of green men.

After eating, we lay down to sleep. This was the beginning of my fifth day on Barsoom and I had not had much rest since I found myself transported to the Valley Dor, the valley beautiful—the valley hideous. A little after noon I woke up to find someone holding my hand and covering it with kisses. With a start I looked up at Thuvia's beautiful face.

"My Prince! My Prince!" she cried, in an ecstasy of happiness. "I thought you were dead. I have mourned you these last several days but my ancestors have been good to me and I see you have survived! I have not lived in vain!"

The girl's voice woke up Xodar and

Carthoris. The boy gazed at the lovely girl in surprise, but she did not notice anyone except me.
She would have thrown her arms around my neck
and smothered me with kisses if I had not gently
stopped her.

"Come, come, Thuvia, you forget yourself,
do you also forget that I am the husband of the
Princess of Helium?"

"I forget nothing, my Prince," she replied.
"You have spoken no word of love to me, nor do
I expect that you ever will; but nothing can prevent me loving you. I would not take the place of
Dejah Thoris. My greatest ambition is to serve
you forever as your slave. No greater blessing
could I ask, no greater honor could I want, no
greater happiness could I hope for."

"When I return to Helium, Thuvia, you shall
come with me, but as an honored equal, and not
as a slave. There you shall find plenty of handsome young nobles who would face Issus herself
to win a smile from you, and we shall have you
married off in short order to one of the best of
them. Forget your foolish infatuation with me,
which your innocence has mistaken for love. I
like your friendship better."

"You are my master; it shall be as you say,"
she replied simply, but there was a note of sadness
in her voice.

"How did you get here, Thuvia? And where
is Tars Tarkas?"

"I fear the great Thark is dead," she replied quietly. "He was a mighty fighter, but a multitude of green warriors overwhelmed him. The last I saw they were carrying him, wounded and bleeding, deeper into the city where they attacked us."

"You are not sure that he is dead? Where is this city?" I demanded.

"It is just beyond this range of hills. The escape vessel you gave us defied our small skill in navigation and we drifted aimlessly for days. Then we decided to abandon the craft and attempt to make our way on foot to the nearest waterway. Yesterday we crossed some hills and came to the dead city. We were walking through the place on one of its back streets when we saw a troop of green warriors approaching.

"Tars Tarkas was leading and they saw him but did not see me. The Thark slipped back and forced me into a doorway, where he told me to remain until I could escape.

"'There will be no escape for me,' he said, 'for these are the Warhoon of the South. When they see my metal we will fight to the death.'

"Then he stepped out to meet them. Ah, my Prince, such fighting! For an hour they swarmed around him, until the Warhoon dead formed a hill where he stood; but at last they overwhelmed him, those behind pushing the ones in front onto him until there was no space for him to swing his sword. Then he stumbled and went down and they rolled over him like a huge wave. When they carried him away toward the heart of the city, I think he was dead—I did not see him move."

"Before we go farther we must be sure," I said. "I cannot leave Tars Tarkas alive among the Warhoons. Tonight I will enter the city and make sure."

"And I will go with you," volunteered Carthoris.

"And I," said Xodar.

"Neither one of you should go," I replied. "It is work that requires stealth and strategy, not force. One man alone may succeed where more would invite disaster. I'll go alone. If I need your help, I will return for you."

They did not like it, but both were good soldiers, and it had been agreed that I would command. The sun was already low, so I did not have long to wait before the sudden darkness of Barsoom engulfed us. With a parting word of instructions to Carthoris and Xodar in case I did not make it back, I set out toward the city.

As I emerged from the hills the nearer moon was making its wild flight through the heavens, its bright beams turning to burnished silver the barbaric splendor of the ancient metropolis. The green hordes that use these deserted cities seldom occupy more than a few blocks around the central plaza. Once I entered the outer streets, I stayed in the shadows. At intersections I halted a moment to make sure that no one was in sight before I ran to the darkness of the opposite side. I made it to the vicinity of the plaza without detection. As I approached the inhabited portion of the city I located the warriors' quarters by the squealing and grunting of the thoats and zitidars corralled in the courtyards.

These familiar sounds, so distinctive of green Martian life, sent a pleasant thrill through me. It was like one might feel coming home after a long absence. It was amid such sounds that I courted Dejah Thoris in the age-old marble halls of the dead city of Korad.

As I stood in the shadows, I saw warriors emerging from several of the buildings. They all went in the same direction, toward a large building that stood in the center of one side of the plaza. My knowledge of green Martian customs convinced me that this was the audience chamber where the Jeddak met his jeds and lesser chieftains. It was obvious that something was going on that might have a bearing on the recent capture of Tars Tarkas. From the animal noises coming from every courtyard around me, I knew that there were many people in the surrounding buildings—probably several communities of the great Warhoon horde of the South.

To pass among all these people without being seen would be a difficult task, but if I was to find the great Thark, it must be done. Nothing interrupted my progress and I got to the Jeddak's headquarters safely. Inside the courtyard a herd of thoats and zitidars moved around restlessly, cropping the moss-like vegetation that covered the area.

I snuck close to the wall, beneath the overhanging balconies of the second floors, until I came to the north end. Here I noted that the first three floors of the building were all lit up, but above that all was dark.

To move through the lighted rooms was out of the question, since they swarmed with green Martian men and women. My only path lay through the upper floors, and to get up to these it was necessary to scale the face of the wall. Getting to the second floor was easy—an agile leap—and in another instant I was on a balcony.

Here, through the windows, I saw the green folk squatting on their sleeping silks and furs, grunting an occasional monosyllable, which, in connection with their telepathic powers, is ample for most of their casual conversations. As I moved closer to listen a warrior entered the room and spoke, "Tan Gama! We are to take the Thark to the Jed for final judgement!"

The warrior addressed got up, beckoned to another fellow squatting nearby to come with them, and all three left the apartment. If I could follow them I might get a chance to free Tars

Tarkas. At least I would learn the location of his prison.

At my right was a door leading from the balcony into the building. It was at the end of a dark hall, and I stepped inside. I saw the three warriors at the other end walking away. A turn to the right took them out of sight as I ran along the hallway in pursuit. My gait was reckless, but I felt that fate had thrown me this opportunity and I could not let it get away.

At the far end of the corridor was a spiral stairway leading to the floors above and below. I was sure, from my knowledge of these ancient buildings and the methods of the Warhoons, that they had gone down to the pits. I myself had once been a prisoner of the cruel hordes of the northern Warhoon, and the memory of my underground dungeon is still vivid. I felt certain that Tars Tarkas lay in a dark cell somewhere beneath the building. Toward the bottom of the stairway the light of a torch revealed the three I was trailing.

Down they went toward the pits beneath the structure, and I followed the flicker of their torch. The way led through a maze of corridors, dark except for the wavering light they carried. We had walked for some time when finally the party turned through a doorway. I ran through the darkness until I reached the point where they left the corridor. There, through the open door,

I saw them removing the chains that secured the Thark to the wall.

Hustling him roughly between them, they immediately came out of the chamber. I managed to run further along the corridor far enough to be outside their light as they emerged from the cell.

I assumed that they would return with Tars Tarkas the same way that they had come, which would have carried them away from me; but to my surprise, they turned in my direction! There was nothing to do but to run on in advance and keep out of the light of their torch. I did not dare stop in any of the intersecting corridors because I did not know the direction they might take.

The sensation of running through these dark passages was awful. I did not know at what moment I might plunge into some terrible pit or meet one of the fearsome creatures that inhabit these lower worlds. The men's torch gave me a little light—just enough to let me guess the direction of the passageways directly in front of me.

Suddenly I came to a place where five corridors came together. I had traveled along one of them for some distance when the faint light of the torch disappeared behind me. I paused to listen for sounds of the party, but the silence was like a tomb.

I realized that the warriors had gone down one of the other corridors with their prisoner, and so I doubled back to take up the much safer position trailing them. But in the darkness, it was necessary to feel every foot of the way back with my hand against the wall so I would not pass the spot where the five passages came together. After what seemed an eternity, I recognized the place by groping across the entrances until I counted the five corridors. But none of them showed the faintest sign of light.

I listened intently, but the naked feet of the green men made no sound, though I thought I heard the clank of side arms in the far distance down one of the corridors. That is the way I went, searching for the light, and stopping to listen occasionally; but soon I was forced to admit I was following a blind lead, as only darkness and silence rewarded my efforts.

I retraced my steps back to wait for the return of the warriors with Tars Tarkas. My knowledge of their customs made me think that he was being escorted to the audience chamber to have his sentence passed and would then be returned to his cell. I did not doubt that they would save the Thark for the sport he would furnish at the Great Games. I leaned against the wall thinking about the awful fix I was in when—what was that?

A faint shuffling noise sounded behind me, and as I cast a glance over my shoulder my blood froze at the sight. It was not so much fear of the present danger as it was the horrifying memories it brought back to me. I nearly went mad in the dungeons of the northern Warhoons when these same blazing eyes came out of the dark and dragged the jailer I had just killed away to their terrible feast.

And now in the black pits of the southern Warhoons I looked into those same fiery eyes, blazing at me through the darkness, revealing no sign of the beast behind them. I think that the most awful thing about these creatures is their silence and the fact that one never sees them— nothing but those eyes glaring out of the dark.

Holding my sword tightly, I backed along the corridor away from the thing, but as I retreated the eyes advanced. On and on I went, but I could not escape my sinister pursuer. Suddenly I heard a shuffling noise at my right, and saw another pair of eyes approaching. As I started my slow retreat again I heard the noise repeated behind me, and then before I could turn I heard it again at my left.

The things were all around me! They had me surrounded at the intersection of two corridors. Retreat was cut off unless I chose to charge one of the beasts. But I had no doubt that the others would attack when I made that move. I could not even guess the size or nature of the weird creatures. But that they were large I knew from the fact that their eyes were level with my own.

Why is it that darkness magnifies our dangers? By day I would have fought any monster on Barsoom, but trapped in the darkness of these silent pits I hesitated. I saw that the matter would soon be taken from my hands, for the eyes all around me were gradually closing in—but still there was that awful silence!

For what seemed like hours the eyes approached closer and closer, until I felt that I would go crazy. I had been turning this way and that to prevent any sudden rush from behind, and I was almost worn out. Finally I could stand it no longer, and turned and charged down on one of my tormentors.

As I was almost on it the thing retreated, but a sound from behind caused me to wheel in time to see three pairs of eyes rushing at me from the rear. With a cry of rage I turned to meet these cowardly beasts, but as I advanced they retreated, too. Another glance over my shoulder discovered the first set of eyes sneaking up on me again. And again I charged, only to see the eyes retreat and hear the muffled rush of the three at my back.

We continued this way for some time but the eyes always seemed a little closer than they were before. They were waiting to spring on my back and I knew it would not be long before they did—I knew I could not endure this repeated charge and countercharge indefinitely. In fact, I could feel myself weakening from the mental and physical strain.

At that moment I caught another glimpse of the single pair of eyes at my back making a sudden rush. I turned to meet the charge and there was a quick attack of the three from the other direction; but I determined to pursue the single pair until I had at least settled one account with these beasts.

There was no sound in the corridor but I knew that the creatures were almost on me. The eyes in front were not retreating as rapidly now and I was almost within sword reach. I raised my sword arm but then felt a heavy body on my back. A cold, moist, slimy thing fastened itself on my neck. I stumbled and went down.

Flight and Pursuit

I could not have been down more than a few seconds, but the next thing I realized was a light shining far off down the corridor and that the eyes were gone. I was unharmed except for a slight bruise on my forehead where I had struck the floor.

I jumped to my feet to check out the light. It came from a torch in a party of four green warriors coming rapidly toward me. They had not seen me so I lost no time slipping into the first side corridor that I could find.

The party came toward the opening where I crouched against the wall. As they passed by I breathed a sigh of relief. I had not been discovered, and best of all, the group consisted of Tars Tarkas and his three guards.

I fell in behind them and soon we were back at his cell. Two of the warriors remained outside while the one with the keys entered with the

Thark to chain him up. The two outside lit a second torch and started to walk back toward their quarters. In a moment they went around a turn in the corridor.

The first torch had been stuck in a socket beside the door, so that its rays lit up both the corridor and the cell. As I saw the two warriors disappear I went up to the cell. I disliked what I had to do but there was no alternative if Tars Tarkas and I were to escape.

I stood outside the cell with my sword ready. I don't like to think about what followed. It is enough that Tars Tarkas was soon wearing the metal of a Warhoon chief and we were hurrying down the corridor following the path of his last two guards.

They were coming back down the circular stairway as the Thark came in view. "Why did you take so long, Tan Gama?" asked one of the men. "We came back to see if you needed help."

"I had trouble with the lock," replied Tars Tarkas as I hid in the shadows, "And now I find that I am missing my dagger! It may be in the Thark's cell. You go on, I'll return to look for it."

"As you wish, Tan Gama," was the reply. "We shall see you directly."

Tars Tarkas turned to retrace his steps to the cell, but he only waited until the two disappeared. Then I joined him, we extinguished the torch, and together we crept toward the stairway.

Cautiously we went up and reached the balcony overlooking the courtyard without being detected. At our right was the window where I had seen Tan Gama and the other warriors. His companions had returned, and we now overheard a portion of their conversation.

"What can be keeping Tan Gama?" asked one.

"He should not take this much time to fetch his dagger," spoke another.

"His dagger?" asked a woman. "What do you mean?"

"Tan Gama left his dagger in the Thark's cell and returned to get it."

"Tan Gama did not wear a dagger tonight," said the woman. "It was broken in today's battle with the Thark, and he gave it to me to repair. See, I have it here," and as she spoke she took out the dagger.

The warriors jumped to their feet and one shouted, "There is something amiss here!"

"That is what I thought when Tan Gama left us at the stairway," said another. "I thought his voice sounded strange."

"Come! To the pits!"

We did not wait to hear any more. Forming my harness into a long single strap, I lowered Tars Tarkas to the courtyard and an instant later dropped to his side. As we reached the courtyard we stood in the shadows beneath the balcony.

"There are now five in our group, Tars Tarkas. Thuvia and ourselves plus a First Born named Xodar and someone you know well, Carthoris of Helium. We will need five thoats to carry us."

"Carthoris!" he cried. "Your son?"

"Yes. I found him in the prison of Shador, on the Sea of Omean, in the land of the First Born."

"I do not know any of these places, John Carter. Are they on Barsoom?"

"On and below, my friend; but wait until we have made our escape, and you will hear a strange story. Now we must steal some thoats and get away to the north before we are discovered."

It is no easy matter to handle thoats, which by nature are as wild and ferocious as their green masters. As we approached they sniffed our unfamiliar scent and circled around us with squeals of rage. They are fearsome appearing brutes at best, but when they are aroused they are fully as dangerous as they look. The thoat stands a good ten feet at the shoulder. His hide is sleek and hairless, and is a dark slate color on his back and sides, shading down his eight legs to a vivid yellow at the huge, padded feet; the belly is pure white. Its gaping mouth, filled with large, sharp teeth, splits its head from its snout to its long massive neck. A broad, flat tail, larger at the tip than the root, completes the picture of this ferocious green Martian mount—a fit war steed for these warlike people.

Thoats are guided by telepathic means so there is no need for reins or bridle, and we tried to find two that would obey our unspoken commands. As they gathered around us we succeeded in mastering them sufficiently to prevent any concerted attack, but the din of their squealing was certain to bring enemy warriors into the courtyard if it continued much longer.

I was successful in reaching the side of one brute, and soon I was seated on his glossy back. A moment later Tars Tarkas had caught and mounted another, and then between us we herded three more toward the gates.

Tars Tarkas rode ahead and, leaning down to the latch, threw the barriers open, while I kept the loose thoats from going back to the herd. Then together we rode into the avenue with our stolen mounts and headed out of the city.

So far our escape had been very lucky and our good fortune did not desert us, for we passed the outer wall of the city and came to our camp without hearing even the faintest sound of pursuit.

Little time was wasted in talking of our adventure. Tars Tarkas and Carthoris exchanged the dignified and formal greetings common on Barsoom, but I could tell that the Thark cared for my boy and that Carthoris felt the same way toward him. Xodar and the green Jeddak were formally introduced to each other. Then Thuvia was lifted to the least wild thoat, Xodar and Carthoris mounted two others, and we set out toward the north. Under the glorious light of the two moons we sped noiselessly across the dead sea bottom, away from the Warhoons and the First Born.

Toward noon the following day we halted to rest. Thuvia volunteered to remain on watch while the balance of the party slept an hour. It seemed to me that I had just closed my eyes when I heard her soft voice warning me of a new danger.

"Arise, O Prince," she whispered. "There is a great body of pursuers behind us."

The girl pointed back from where we had come and I thought that I could see a thin dark line on the far horizon. I awoke Tars Tarkas, whose giant stature towered high above the rest of us and could see the farthest.

"It is a large body of mounted men," he said, "and they are traveling at high speed."

There was no time to be lost. We mounted our thoats, turned our faces once more toward the north and took flight again. For the rest of the day and all the following night we raced across the wilderness. Slowly but surely they were gaining on us. Just before dark they were close enough for us to plainly see that they were green Martians, and all during the long night we heard them behind us. As the sun came up it showed the pursuing horde just a quarter-mile behind. As they saw us a fiendish shout of triumph came from their ranks.

Several miles in front of us was a range of hills—the far shore of the dead sea we had been crossing. If we could reach these hills our chances of escape would be better, but Thuvia's mount was showing signs of exhaustion. I was riding beside her when suddenly her animal staggered and lurched against mine. I saw that he was going down, so I snatched the girl from his back and swung her behind me.

This double burden soon proved too much for my beast, and the group had to slow down. In that little party there was not one who would desert another; yet we were from different countries, different colors, different races, different religions—and one of us was from a different world.

We were close to the hills, but the Warhoons were gaining so rapidly that we had given up hope of reaching them. Thuvia and I were in the rear—our beast was lagging behind more and more. Suddenly I felt the girl's warm lips press a kiss on my shoulder. "For thy sake, O my Prince," she murmured. Then her arms let go of my waist and she was gone!

I turned and saw that she had slipped to the ground in front of the green demons, thinking that by lightening the burden of my mount it might be able to carry me to safety. Poor child! She should have known John Carter better than that.

Turning my thoat, I urged him back, hoping to reach her side. Carthoris must have glanced behind and taken in the situation, for by the time I reached Thuvia he was there, too. Springing from his mount, he threw the damsel up on its back. Turning the animal's head toward the hills, he gave the beast a sharp crack across the rump with the flat of his sword and off they went.

The brave boy's act of self-sacrifice filled me with pride, and I did not care that it had cost us our last chance for escape. The Warhoons were now close. Tars Tarkas and Xodar had discovered our absence and were charging back to support us. Everything pointed toward a splendid ending of my second journey to Barsoom! I hated to go out without having held my divine princess in my arms once again, but if it was not in the Book of Fate then I would take what was coming to me.

Since Carthoris was not mounted, I slipped from my mount and took my place at his side to meet the charge of the howling devils. A moment later Tars Tarkas and Xodar were on either side of us. They also turned their thoats loose so that we were all on an equal footing.

The Warhoons were a hundred yards from us when a loud report sounded behind us and a moment later an explosion burst in their ranks. At once all was confusion. A hundred warriors toppled to the ground. Riderless thoats plunged among the dead and dying. Dismounted warriors were trampled underfoot in the stampede. All semblance of order left the ranks of the green men, and as they looked above our heads to trace the origin of this unexpected attack, disorder turned to retreat and retreat to wild panic. In another moment they were racing away from us.

We turned back to look at where the noise had come from and saw a battleship swinging majestically through the air. Her bow gun spoke again as we looked, and another shell burst among the fleeing Warhoons. As she drew nearer I could not repress a wild cry of elation as I saw the flag of Helium waving on her bow!

Under Arrest

As we stood gazing at the magnificent vessel, we saw a second and then a third float over the top of the hills. A squadron of one-man air scouts was launching from the upper decks of the nearer vessel, and in a moment they were speeding in long, swift dives down to the ground.

Warriors surrounded us and an officer stepped forward. When he saw Carthoris he placed his hands on the boy's shoulder, and said, "Carthoris, my Prince! Kaor! Kaor! Hor Vastus greets the son of Dejah Thoris, Princess of Helium, and of her husband, John Carter. Where have you been, O my Prince? All Helium has been in sorrow. Terrible disasters have fallen on our nation since the day you left us!"

"Do not grieve, my good Hor Vastus. I do not return by myself to cheer my mother's heart and the hearts of my beloved people! I also bring the one who all Barsoom loves—her greatest warrior and her savior—John Carter, Prince of Helium!"

Hor Vastus turned and as his eyes fell on me he almost collapsed from surprise. "John Carter!" he exclaimed, and then a sudden troubled look came into his eyes. "My Prince . . . where have you . . ." and then he stopped, but I knew the question that he dared not ask. The loyal fellow would not be the one to force the confession that I had returned from the River Iss, the River of Mystery, back from the shore of the Lost Sea of Korus, and the Valley Dor.

"Ah, my Prince," he continued, as though no thought had interrupted his greeting, "that you are back is sufficient, and let my sword have the honor of being first at your feet." With these words the noble fellow unbuckled his scabbard and flung his sword on the ground at my feet.

If you knew the customs and the character of red Martians you would appreciate the depth of meaning that simple act conveyed to me and to everyone around us. The thing was equivalent to saying, "My sword, my body, my life, my soul are yours to do with as you wish. Until death and after death I look to you alone for authority for my every act. Be you right or wrong, your word shall be my only truth. Whoever raises his hand against you must answer to me and my sword."

It is the oath of fealty that men occasionally

pay to a Jeddak whose character and chivalrous acts have inspired the love of his followers. There was only one response possible. I lifted the sword from the ground, raised the hilt to my lips, and then, stepping to Hor Vastus, I buckled the weapon back on him with my own hands.

"Hor Vastus," I said, placing my hand on his shoulder, "I will never call on you to draw this sword except in the cause of truth, justice, and righteousness."

As we spoke a larger aircraft was launched from above and landed near us. As she touched down, an officer saluted Hor Vastus and said, "Kantos Kan desires that this party be brought to the deck of the Xavarian."

As we approached the craft I looked around and noticed that Thuvia was missing! No one had seen her since Carthoris had sent her and her thoat galloping toward the hills. Hor Vastus immediately dispatched a dozen air scouts to search for her. It was not possible that she had gone far. We others boarded the craft, and a moment later were on the Xavarian.

The first man to greet me was Kantos Kan himself. My old friend had been promoted to the highest place in Helium's navy, but to me he was still the same brave warrior who had shared the horrors of a Warhoon dungeon, the atrocities of the Great Games, and dangers in the hostile city of Zodanga during our search for Dejah Thoris.

At that time I had been an unknown wanderer on a strange planet, and he a simple lieutenant in the navy of Helium. Today he commanded all Helium's great terrors of the skies, and I was a Prince of the House of Tardos Mors, Jeddak of Helium.

He did not ask me where I had been. Like Hor Vastus, he too dreaded the truth and would not be the one to cause me to say something incriminating. But he seemed satisfied to know that I was with him once more. He greeted Carthoris and Tars Tarkas with delight, but he did not ask them where they had been either. He looked at me and said, "You do not know how we of Helium love this son of yours. It is as though all the love we bore his father and poor mother had been centered in him. When it became known that he was lost, ten million people wept."

"What do you mean by 'his poor mother'?" I whispered, for his words carried a sinister meaning.

He drew me to one side and explained, "For a year, ever since Carthoris disappeared, Dejah Thoris has grieved and mourned for her lost boy. The blow of years ago, when you did not return from the atmosphere plant, was lessened to some extent by the duties of motherhood, for your son broke his shell that very night."

"That she suffered terribly, all Helium knew, for all Helium suffered with her the loss of her prince! But with the boy gone there was nothing left for her, and after expedition upon expedition returned with no clue as to his whereabouts, our beloved princess drooped lower and lower, until all who saw her felt that it would be just a matter of days before she went to join her loved ones down the River Iss to the Valley Dor.

"As a last resort, Mors Kajak, her father, and Tardos Mors, her grandfather, took command of two mighty expeditions, and sailed away a month ago to explore every inch of ground in the northern hemisphere of Barsoom. For two weeks no word has come back from them, and there are rumors that they met with a terrible disaster and that all are dead.

"About this time Zat Arras renewed his demands for the hand of Dejah Thoris in marriage. He has been after her since you disappeared. She hated and feared him, but with both her father and grandfather gone, Zat Arras was very powerful, for he is still Jed of Zodanga. I am sure you remember Tardos Mors appointed him to that position after you refused the honor.

"He had a secret audience with her six days ago. No one knows what took place, but the next day Dejah Thoris disappeared, and with her a dozen of her household guard and body servants, including Sola the green woman. They left no word of their intentions, but it is always that way with those who go on the pilgrimage from which no one returns. We cannot think of anything except that Dejah Thoris has started on the journey down to the River Iss, and that her devoted servants have chosen to go with her.

"Zat Arras was at Helium when she disappeared. He commands this fleet that has been searching for her. We have found no trace of her and I fear our quest may be in vain."

While we talked, Hor Vastus' searchers were returning to the Xavarian. Not one had discovered a trace of Thuvia. I was much depressed over the disappearance of Dejah Thoris and now the fate of Thuvia was added to my burdens. I believed she was once the daughter of some proud Barsoomian house, and I wanted her to be safe and comfortable in Helium. I was about to ask that the search be continued when a flier from the flagship arrived with a message from Zat Arras.

My friend read the dispatch and then turned to me, "Zat Arras commands me to bring our 'prisoners' to him. There is nothing I can do—he is the current supreme ruler in Helium. It would be far more in keeping with chivalry and good taste if he were to come here and greet the savior of Barsoom with the honors that are his due."

"You know full well, my friend," I said, smiling, "that Zat Arras has good cause to hate me. Nothing would please him better than to have me killed. Now that he has such a good excuse, let us go and see if he has the courage to try it."

Summoning Carthoris, Tars Tarkas, and Xodar, we entered the small flier with Kantos Kan, and in a moment were stepping to the deck of the evil jed's flagship.

As we approached the Jed of Zodanga, no sign of greeting or recognition crossed his face; he did not even acknowledge Carthoris. His attitude was cold, haughty, and uncompromising.

"Kaor, Zat Arras," I said in greeting, but he did not respond.

"Why were these prisoners not disarmed?" he asked Kantos Kan.

"They are not prisoners, Zat Arras," replied the officer. "Two of them are of Helium's noblest family. Tars Tarkas, Jeddak of Thark, is Tardos Mor's most beloved ally. The other is a friend and companion of the Prince of Helium— that is enough to know."

"It is not enough for me, however," snapped Zat Arras. "I must hear more from those who have taken the pilgrimage than just their names. Where have you been, John Carter?"

"I have just come from the Valley Dor and the Land of the First Born, Zat Arras," I replied.

"Ah!" he exclaimed in evident pleasure, "you do not deny it, then? You have returned from the River Iss and the Valley Dor?"

"I have come back from a land of false hope, from a valley of torture and death. With my com-

panions I have escaped from the hideous clutches of lying fiends. I have come back to the
Barsoom that I saved from death years ago to
save her again, but this time from death in its
most frightful form."

"Cease, sinner!" cried Zat Arras. "Do not
hope to save your cowardly carcass by inventing
horrid lies to—" but he got no further. One does
not call John Carter "coward" and "liar" lightly,
and Zat Arras should have known better. Before
anyone could stop me, I was at his side and with
one hand grabbed his throat.

"If I come from heaven or hell, Zat Arras,
you will find me the same John Carter that I have
always been. No man can say such things to me!"
And with that I commenced to bend him back
across my knee and tighten my grip on his throat.

"Seize him!" squeaked Zat Arras, and a
dozen officers sprang forward to assist him.

Kantos Kan came close and whispered to me,
"Stop, I beg of you! It will involve us all, for we
will not allow these men to lay hands on you
without coming to your aid. My officers and men
will join me and we will have a mutiny that may
lead to revolution. For the sake of Tardos Mors
and Helium, please desist."

At his words I released Zat Arras and, turning my back on him, walked toward the ship's
rail. "Come, Kantos Kan," I said, "the Prince of
Helium wishes to return to the Xavarian."

No one interfered. Zat Arras stood white and trembling among his officers. Some of them looked at him with scorn and drew toward me, while one, a man long in the service and confidence of Tardos Mors, spoke to me in a low tone as I passed him, "You may count my metal among your fighting-men, John Carter."

I thanked him and passed on. In silence we disembarked, and soon stepped once more on the Xavarian. Fifteen minutes later we received orders from the flagship to proceed toward Helium.

Our journey was uneventful. Carthoris and I were wrapped in the gloomiest of thoughts about Dejah Thoris. Kantos Kan worried about what might happen to Helium if Zat Arras tried to enforce the laws that demanded death for any fugitives from the Valley Dor. Tars Tarkas grieved for the loss of his daughter. Xodar alone was carefree—a fugitive and outlaw, he could be no worse off in Helium than anywhere else.

"Let us hope that we go out with good red blood on our blades," was all Xodor could say to our somber group. It was a simple wish and the one most likely to be granted.

I noticed the officers of the Xavarian dividing into two factions. There were those who gathered around Carthoris and myself, while an equal number did not come near us. The second group was most likely bound by their belief in the doctrine of the Valley Dor and River Iss and Sea of

Korus. I did not blame them, for I knew how a strong religious belief could affect an otherwise intelligent people.

By returning from the Valley Dor we had committed the most outrageous sin; by recounting our adventures and stating the facts as they existed we were an outrage to the centuries old religion of their fathers. We were evil devils— heretics. Even those who still followed us from personal love and loyalty did so despite the fact that they would be judged as well. It is very hard to accept a new religion, no matter how alluring its promises may be. But to reject an old religion as a falsehood without being offered anything to take its place is a most difficult thing to ask.

Kantos Kan did not want to talk about our experiences among the Therns and the First Born. "It is enough," he said, "that I jeopardize my life here and in the hereafter by being with you at all—do not ask me to add to my sins by listening to heresy."

I knew that sooner or later the time must come when our friends and enemies would be forced to declare themselves openly. When we reached Helium there would be an accounting, and I feared the ill will of Zat Arras would weigh heavily against us, for he represented the government of Helium. To take sides against him was equivalent to treason. The majority of the troops would follow the lead of their officers, and I knew that many of the most powerful men of both the land and air forces would join John Carter in the face of god, man, or devil.

On the other hand, some of the common people might demand that we pay the penalty of our sacrilege. The outlook seemed dark from whatever angle I viewed it, but I was so worried about Dejah Thoris that I gave Helium's problems hardly a thought.

In my mind were the frightful dangers that I knew my princess might even now be facing—the horrid plant men—the ferocious white apes—slavery under the Therns—capture by the First Born—servant of Issus. At times I covered my face with my hands to try to shut out the fearful thoughts from my mind.

We eventually arrived at the mile-high scarlet tower that marks greater Helium from her twin city. As we descended, a large crowd could be seen surging in the streets. Helium had been notified by radio of our approach.

Carthoris, Tars Tarkas, Xodar, and I were transferred to the roof of the Temple of Reward, so that we did not pass among the people at all. I knew that Zat Arras did not trust the people to be near us. He feared that their love for us might break into a demonstration that would wipe out their superstitious horror of our "crime." I could not guess his plans, but that they were sinister was plain to see.

We were lodged in a room overlooking the Avenue of Ancestors down which we could see to the Gate of Jeddaks, five miles away. Hundreds of thousands of people packed the plaza in front of the temple and the crowd stretched for miles down the avenue. They were very orderly but when they saw us at the window they cheered for hours.

It was late in the afternoon that Zat Arras sent a messenger to inform us that we would be tried in the great hall of the temple early the next day.

CHAPTER
17

The Death Sentence

A few moments before the appointed time, ten officers of the guard appeared at our quarters to take us to the trial.

We entered the chamber, surrounded by our armed guards, and marched down the broad Aisle of Hope, as it is called, to the platform in the center. Three solid ranks of Zodangan soldiers lined either side of the aisle from the entrance to the rostrum. The vast coliseum was packed to its full capacity. All classes were represented—all ages, and both sexes. The hum of conversation ceased and when we reached the platform, or Throne of Righteousness, the silence of death enveloped the ten thousand spectators.

I saw our judges up on the platform. As is the custom on Barsoom, there were thirty-one, supposedly selected by lot from men of the noble class. But to my amazement, I did not see a single friendly face. Practically all were Zodangans, and it was I who orchestrated Zodanga's defeat at the hands of the green hordes and her subsequent domination by Helium. There would be little justice here for John Carter, or his son, or for the great Thark who had commanded the savage tribesmen who overran Zodanga's broad avenues, looting, burning, and murdering.

The judges were seated around the edge of the circular platform. We were assigned seats with our backs toward a small platform in the exact center of the larger one. This placed us facing the judges and the audience. Each of us would take his place on the smaller platform while his case was being heard.

Zat Arras himself sat in the golden chair of the presiding magistrate. As we were seated, he stood up and called my name. "John Carter, take your place on the Pedestal of Truth to be judged according to your acts. Here you will know the reward you have earned by your actions."

Then turning to the audience, he read the charges against me. "Know you, O judges and people of Helium, that John Carter, one time Prince of Helium, has come back to your fair city and by his own statement has returned from the Valley Dor and even from the Temple of Issus itself.

"Know that, in the presence of many men of Helium, he has sinned against the sacred River Iss, and against the Valley Dor, and the Lost Sea of Korus, and the Holy Therns themselves, and even against Issus, Goddess of Death, and of Life Eternal.

"And know you further by your own eyes that see him here now upon the Pedestal of Truth that he has indeed returned from these sacred places in spite of our customs, and in violation of our ancient religion.

"He who is once dead may not live again. He who attempts it must be made dead for ever. Judges, your duty lies plain before you—there can be no testimony here except the truth. What reward shall be given to John Carter in accordance with the acts he has committed?"

There was a slight pause and then one of the judges shouted, "Death!"

Suddenly a man jumped to his feet in the audience, and raising his hand, cried: "Justice! Justice! Justice!" It was Kantos Kan, and as all eyes turned toward him he leaped past the Zodangan soldiers and ran up onto the platform.

"What manner of justice is this?" he shouted at Zat Arras. "The defendant has not been heard, nor has he had an opportunity to call others in his behalf. In the name of the people of Helium, I demand fair and impartial treatment for the Prince of Helium."

A great cry arose from the audience: "Justice! Justice! Justice!" and Zat Arras did not dare deny them.

"Speak, then," he snarled, turning to me; "but do not insult our religion or the customs that are sacred on Barsoom."

"Men of Helium," I cried, turning to the spectators, and speaking over the heads of my judges, "how can John Carter expect justice from the men of Zodanga? He cannot! It is to the men of Helium that he makes his case!

"It is not in his own cause that he speaks now—it is in your cause—in the cause of your wives and daughters, and of wives and daughters yet unborn. It is to save THEM from the unthinkably atrocious indignities that I have seen heaped on the fair women of Barsoom in the place men call the Temple of Issus.

"It is to save YOU ALL from the sucking embrace of the plant men, from the fangs of the great white apes, and from the cruelty of the Holy Therns. The cold, dead River Iss carries you to these horrors from homes of love and life and happiness.

"There is no man here who does not know the history of John Carter. How he came among you from another world and rose from a prisoner among the green men, through torture and persecution, to a place high among the highest of Barsoom. Never did you know John Carter to lie in his own behalf, or to say anything that might harm the people of Barsoom. Never has he been heard to speak lightly of your religion which he respected without understanding.

"There can be no man here, or anywhere on Barsoom, who does not owe his life to a single act of mine, in which I sacrificed myself and the happiness of my princess so that you might live. And so, men of Helium, I think that I have the right to demand that I be heard AND that I be believed! Let me save you from the false hereafter of the Valley Dor and Issus as I saved you from death on that other day.

"It is to you of Helium that I speak now. When I am done let the men of Zodanga have their will with me. Zat Arras has taken my sword from me, so the men of Zodanga no longer fear me. Will you listen?"

"Speak, John Carter, Prince of Helium!" cried a powerful noble from the audience, and the multitude echoed him, until the building rocked with the noise of their demonstration.

Zat Arras knew better than to interfere with such sentiment as was expressed that day in the Temple of Reward, and so for the next two hours I talked with the people of Helium.

But when I finished, Zat Arras got up, turned to the judges, and said in a low tone: "My nobles, you have heard John Carter's plea; every opportunity has been given him to prove his innocence; but instead he has utilized the time to make further insults against our religion. What, gentlemen, is your verdict?"

"Death to the sinner!" cried one, springing to his feet, and in an instant the entire thirty-one judges were on their feet shouting in agreement.

If the people did not hear Zat Arras' charges, they certainly heard the verdict of the tribunal. A sullen murmur rose louder and louder through the packed coliseum, and then Kantos Kan, who had not left the platform since he had taken his place near me, raised his hand for silence. When he could be heard he spoke to the people in a cool and level voice.

"You have heard the fate that the men of Zodanga would give to Helium's noblest hero and the leader of the army that conquered their city. It may be the duty of the men of Helium to accept the verdict as final—or it may not. Let each man act according to his own heart. Here is the answer of Kantos Kan, head of the navy of Helium," and with that he unbuckled his scabbard and threw his sword at my feet.

In an instant soldiers and citizens, officers and nobles were crowding past the soldiers of Zodanga and forcing their way to the Throne of Righteousness. A hundred men surged onto the platform, and a hundred blades rattled and clanked to the floor at my feet. Zat Arras and his officers were furious, but they were helpless. One by one I raised the swords to my lips and buckled them back on their owners.

"Come," said Kantos Kan, "we will escort

John Carter and his party to his palace," and they formed ranks around us and started toward the stairs leading to the Aisle of Hope.

"Stop!" cried Zat Arras. "Soldiers of Zodanga, let no prisoner leave the Throne of Righteousness!"

The Zodanga soldiers were the only organized body of troops inside the temple, so Zat Arras was confident that his orders would be obeyed, but he did not anticipate the opposition that rose up to meet his advancing soldiers.

From every quarter of the coliseum swords flashed and men rushed the Zodangans. Someone raised a cry: "Tardos Mors is dead—a thousand years to John Carter, Jeddak of Helium!" As I heard that and saw the ugly attitude of the men of Helium toward the Zodangan soldiers, I knew that only a miracle could stop a clash that would end in civil war.

"Hold!" I cried, leaping to the Pedestal of Truth. "Let no man move! A single sword thrust here today could plunge Helium into a bloody war with results no one can foresee! It will turn brother against brother and father against son. No man's life is worth that sacrifice. I would rather submit to the biased judgment of Zat Arras than cause civil strife in Helium!

"Let us each give a little, and let this matter rest until Tardos Mors or his son returns. If neither is back at the end of a year a second trial should be held." I turned to Zat Arras and said in a low voice, "Unless you are a bigger fool than I think, you will grab the chance I am offering you before it is too late. Once that multitude of swords is drawn against your guards no one can stop the consequences. What do you say? Speak quickly!"

Zat Arras raised his voice to the angry sea around us, "Stay your hands, men of Helium! The sentence of the court is passed, but the day of retribution has not been set. I, Zat Arras, Jed of Zodanga, appreciating the royal connections of the prisoner and his past services to Helium and Barsoom, grant a respite of one year, or until the return of Mors Kajak or Tardos Mors. Disperse quietly!"

No one moved. Instead, they stood in tense silence with their eyes on me, like they were waiting for a signal to attack.

"Clear the temple," commanded Zat Arras, in a low tone to one of his officers.

Fearing the result of an attempt to carry out this order by force, I stepped to the edge of the platform and, pointing toward the main entrance, asked the multitude to go out peacefully. They turned at my request and filed past the soldiers in a silent and threatening mass.

Kantos Kan and the others who had sworn allegiance stayed back with me. He said, "We will escort you to your palace, my Prince. Come,

Carthoris and Xodar. Come, Tars Tarkas." And with a sneer at Zat Arras, he turned and walked up the Aisle of Hope. The four of us walked behind him, followed by my hundred loyal followers. No hand was raised to stop us, though hostile eyes followed our triumphal march.

In the avenue we found crowds of people, but they opened a path for us, and many swords were flung at my feet as I passed through the city toward my palace. Once there my old slaves fell on their knees and kissed my hands as I greeted them. They did not care where I had been. It was enough that I had returned.

"Ah, master," cried one, "if our divine princess were here this would be a wonderful day indeed."

Tears came to my eyes and I was forced to turn away to hide my emotions. Carthoris wept openly as the slaves pressed around him with expressions of affection and words of sorrow for our common loss.

The Prince of Helium's palace dining hall held a sad feast of welcome that evening. We were over a hundred strong, not counting the members of my little court, for Dejah Thoris and I had maintained a household consistent with our royal rank.

The feast table, according to red Martian custom, was triangular. Carthoris and I presided in the center of two of the three sides—midway on the third side stood Dejah Thoris' high-backed chair. It was vacant except for her gorgeous wedding trappings and jewels. A slave stood behind it ready to do her bidding the same as when his mistress had occupied her place. It was the way on Barsoom, so I endured the anguish, though it broke my heart to see that silent chair where there should have been my laughing and vivacious princess.

At my right sat Kantos Kan, while to the right of Dejah Thoris' empty place was Tars Tarkas. The place of honor at a Martian feast is on the right side of the hostess, and this place was always reserved for the Thark when he visited. On these occasions we provided him with a large chair and dining platform suitable to his immense stature.

Hor Vastus sat in the seat of honor on the right side of Carthoris. There was little general conversation. It was a quiet and sad party. The loss of Dejah Thoris was still fresh in our mind, and to this was added fear for the safety of Tardos Mors and Mors Kajak. Helium's fate, should it prove true that we had permanently lost our Jeddak, was a concern for all of us.

Suddenly our attention was attracted by the sound of a crowd of people shouting outside. A slave rushed into the dining hall yelling, "Dejah Thoris is found! A messenger from Dejah Thoris!"

I did not wait to hear anymore. With a single leap I cleared the table and ran to the balcony. I dropped to the ground and ran toward the advancing party which surrounded a wild thoat and rider. As I came near I saw that the figure on the thoat was Sola and I shouted, "Where is the Princess of Helium?"

The green girl slid from her mount and came toward me. "O my Prince! My Prince! She is gone forever. The black pirates of Barsoom have stolen her!"

CHAPTER 18

Sola's Story

After Sola greeted her father, she told the story of the pilgrimage and capture of Dejah Thoris: "Seven days ago, after her audience with Zat Arras, Dejah Thoris tried to leave the palace in the dead of night. I knew that something awful was troubling her and when I saw her sneaking out of the palace I did not need to be told her destination.

"I quickly gathered a dozen of her most faithful guards and explained my fears to them. They volunteered to follow our beloved princess in her wanderings, even to the sacred River Iss and the Valley Dor. We found her and Woola, the hound, a short distance from the palace. She ordered us back, but we disobeyed her, and when she found that we would not let her go on alone, she wept and embraced us, and together we went out into the night toward the south.

"The following day we found a herd of small thoats, and after that we were mounted and made good time. We traveled due south until the morning of the fifth day when we sighted a fleet of battleships sailing north. We attempted to hide but they spotted us and soon we were surrounded by a horde of black men. The brave men of our guard fought to the end, but they were soon overcome and slain. Only Dejah Thoris and I were spared. We were tied up and taken aboard one of the pirate ships.

"The fleet continued north after our capture. That evening one of the smaller scout cruisers returned with a prisoner—a young red woman they picked up under the very noses of three red Martian battleships. After interrogation by the commander she was put in the compartment with us.

"The new captive told us that she had taken the voluntary pilgrimage from the court of her father, the Jeddak of Ptarth. She was Thuvia, the Princess of Ptarth. When she heard the name Dejah Thoris, she fell on her knees. She told your lady that she had been with John Carter, Prince of Helium, and Carthoris, her son, that very morning.

"Dejah Thoris had trouble believing her, but after the girl told us some of the strange and harrowing adventures that occurred since meeting John Carter, she knew that it had to be the Prince of Helium. She said, 'For who, other than John Carter, could have done these deeds?' And when Thuvia told Dejah Thoris of her love for John Carter, and his loyalty and devotion to the princess of his choice, Dejah Thoris broke down and wept. She cursed Zat Arras and the cruel fate that had driven her from Helium just days before the return of her beloved lord.

"The princess told her, 'I do not blame you for loving him, Thuvia. I know that your affection for him is pure and sincere.'

"The fleet continued north almost to the border of Helium, but they realized that John Carter had indeed escaped them and so they turned south once more. Shortly after the course change a guard entered and dragged me to the deck.

"'There is no place in the Land of the First Born for a green one,' he said, and with that he shoved me off the deck of the battleship. This was the easiest way of ridding the vessel of my presence and killing me at the same time.

"But fate intervened, and by a miracle I escaped with only bruises. To my surprise, as I went overboard into the darkness I landed on a soft mass of vegetation not twenty feet from the deck of the ship!

"I lay all night where I had fallen and the next morning I saw what had saved me from a terrible death. As the sun rose I viewed a vast panorama of sea bottom lying far below me. I was in the top of a tall tree on the highest hill of the range of hills bordering this low area. In the darkness the fleet had barely cleared the crest of the hills, and at that instant the guard threw me off the ship.

"A settlement was a few miles west of me. When I reached it I found to my delight that it belonged to Helium. They supplied me with a thoat—the rest you know."

For many minutes no one spoke. Dejah Thoris in the clutches of the First Born! I shuddered at the thought, but all of a sudden the old fire of unconquerable self-confidence surged through me. I jumped to my feet, and with upraised sword took a solemn vow to reach, rescue, and revenge my princess.

A hundred swords leaped from a hundred scabbards, and a hundred fighting-men sprang up and pledged their lives and fortunes to my expedition. Already my plans were formulated. I thanked each loyal friend, and leaving Carthoris to entertain them, withdrew to a private chamber with Kantos Kan, Tars Tarkas, Xodar, and Hor Vastus.

Here we discussed the details of the expedition until long after dark. Xodar was positive that Issus would choose both Dejah Thoris and Thuvia to be her servants, and added "for that year they will be comparatively safe and we will know where to look for them."

In the matter of equipping a fleet to enter

Omean, the details were left to Kantos Kan and Xodar. Kantos Kan was to obtain the vessels we required as rapidly as possible, and Xodar would direct their refitting with water propellers. For many years Xodar had been in charge of the refitting of captured battleships so they could navigate the Sea of Omean. He was familiar with the construction of the propellers, housings, and the auxiliary gearing required.

It was estimated that six months were needed to complete our preparations. Of course, the utmost secrecy must be maintained to keep the project from the ears of Zat Arras. Kantos Kan was sure that nothing short of the title of Jeddak of Helium would satisfy him. He said, "I doubt if he would even welcome the return of Dejah Thoris, for it would mean someone else nearer the throne. With you and Carthoris out of the way there would be little to prevent him from assuming the title of Jeddak."

"There is a way, to stop him completely and for ever," whispered Hor Vastus.

"What?" I asked.

He smiled and said, "I'll whisper it here, but some day I will stand on the dome of the Temple of Reward and shout it to cheering multitudes."

"What do you mean?" asked Kantos Kan.

"John Carter, Jeddak of Helium," said Hor Vastus in a low voice.

The eyes of my companions lit up and grim

smiles of anticipation spread over their faces. But I shook my head, smiled and said, "No, my friends. I thank you, but it cannot be. Not yet, at least. When we know that Tardos Mors and Mors Kajak will not return, then we can talk. Then I shall join you all to see that the people of Helium choose their next Jeddak. Who they choose may count on the loyalty of my sword. Until then Tardos Mors is Jeddak of Helium, and Zat Arras is his representative."

"As you will, John Carter," said Hor Vastus, "but—What was that?" he whispered, pointing toward the window overlooking the gardens.

The words were barely out of his mouth before he leaped out onto the balcony.

"There he goes!" he cried excitedly. "Guards! Over there! Guards!"

We were close behind him and saw a man run across the lawn and disappear into the shrubbery beyond.

"He was on the balcony when I first saw him," cried Hor Vastus. "Quick! Follow him!"

Together we ran to the gardens, but though we scoured the grounds with the entire guard for hours, we could find no trace of the night marauder.

"What do you make of it, Kantos Kan?" asked Tars Tarkas.

"A spy sent by Zat Arras," he replied. "That is his way."

"He will have something interesting to report to his master," said Hor Vastus.

"I hope he heard only our references to a new Jeddak. If he overheard our plans to rescue Dejah Thoris, it will mean civil war, for he will attempt to foil us, and I will not be stopped. I will go through with these plans to save my princess even if it throws Helium into a bloody conflict. Nothing but death will stop me, and if I die, my friends, will you take an oath to continue the search and bring her back to her grand-father's court?"

They all held up their swords and swore to rescue my princess or die in the attempt.

It was agreed that the battleships should go to Hastor to be refitted. This was another of Helium's cities, far to the southwest. Because Kantos Kan was commander-in-chief of the navy, he had the power to order the vessels to go there. After the work he could assign the ships to remote parts of the empire until we were ready to assemble for the attack on Omean.

It was late that night before our conference broke up, but each man had his particular duties outlined, and the details of the entire plan had been mapped out.

Kantos Kan and Xodar were to attend to the ships. Tars Tarkas was to go to Thark and assem-ble a horde of green warriors who would travel in transports directly to the Valley Dor and the

Temple of Issus. The newly fitted fleet was to enter Omean and destroy the vessels of the First Born.

Hor Vastus had the delicate mission of organizing a secret force of red fighting-men. We estimated that it would require over a million men to operate the thousand ships we intended to use.

After they left I said goodnight to Carthoris. I was very tired and lay down on my sleeping silks looking forward to the first good night's sleep since I returned to Barsoom. But I was to be disappointed.

I do not know how long I slept but when I awoke it was to find a gag in my mouth and my arms and legs securely bound. Six burly men were standing over me and they had worked so quickly that by the time I was awake I could not resist them.

They never spoke a word, and the gag prevented me from speaking. They carried me out into the corridor and then through a secret panel and down to the passageways beneath my palace. After a while we stopped and a second later I was pushed into a chamber. Three men, richly adorned in the most exquisite trappings, stared down at me from a high bench. One of them, with a mocking smile on his thin, cruel lips, was Zat Arras.

Black Despair

"**A**h, to what do I owe the pleasure of this unexpected visit from the Prince of Helium?" the Zodangian said sarcastically.

One of the guards removed the gag from my mouth, but I did not reply to Zat Arras. I stood there in silence with my level gaze fixed on the Jed of Zodanga. The eyes of those in the room were fixed first on me and then on Zat Arras, until finally a flush of anger crept over his face.

"You may go," he said to my kidnappers, and when only four of us were left in the chamber, he spoke to me again in a voice of ice—very slowly and deliberately, like he was carefully choosing his words.

"John Carter, by the edict of custom, by the law of our religion, and by the verdict of an impartial court, you are condemned to die. The people cannot save you—I alone am able to accomplish that. You are absolutely in my power to do with as I wish—I may kill you, or I may free you, and should I decide to kill you, no one would be the wiser.

"You may go free now on one condition. We know that Tardos Mors will never return to Helium. Neither will Mors Kajak, nor Dejah Thoris. Helium must select a new jeddak within the year AND I WILL BE the Jeddak of Helium. Say that you will take up my cause. This is the price of your freedom. I am done."

I knew he could destroy me, and if I was dead there was little doubt that he would easily become Jeddak of Helium. Free, I could carry on the search for Dejah Thoris. But if I was dead, my brave comrades might not be able to carry out our plans. So, by refusing to consent to his request, I could not stop him from becoming Jeddak and I would doom Dejah Thoris to the horrors of Issus.

For a moment I was perplexed, but for a moment only. The proud daughter of a thousand Jeddaks would choose death to a dishonorable alliance such as this. Certainly, I could not do less for Helium.

I faced Zat Arras and said, "There can be no alliance between a traitor to Helium and a Prince of the House of Tardos Mors. I do not believe that the great Jeddak is dead."

Zat Arras shrugged his shoulders and said, "Soon your opinions will be of interest to no one, so make the best of them while you can. I will permit you to reflect on my magnanimous offer. You will go to the silence and darkness of the pits to think about this proposal. Take with you the knowledge that if you fail to agree you will never emerge again."

Zat Arras clapped his hands as he ceased speaking. The guards entered and he waved his hand in my direction and said, "To the pits." That was all. Four men dragged me from the chamber, and escorted me through interminable tunnels, down, ever down beneath the city of Helium.

They halted in a fair-sized chamber where, by torchlight, I saw chains fastened to the rocky walls. At the ends of many of the chains were human skeletons. One of these they kicked aside, and, unlocking a huge padlock that had once secured a human ankle, they snapped the iron band around my leg. Then they went off, taking the light with them.

I was left in darkness. For a few minutes I could hear them walking, but even this grew fainter and fainter, until at last the silence was as complete as the darkness. I was alone with my gruesome companions—with the bones of dead men whose fate was a sign of what might happen to me. I do not know how long I stood listening in the darkness, but the silence was unbroken, and at last I dropped to the floor and slept.

It must have been several hours later that I awoke to find a young man standing in front of me. In one hand he held a light, in the other a bowl containing a gruel-like mixture—the common prison fare of Barsoom.

"My name is Parthak. Zat Arras sends you greetings, and commands me to inform you that although he is fully aware of the plot to make you Jeddak of Helium, he is not inclined to withdraw his offer to you. To gain your freedom you must accept the terms of his proposition."

I shook my head. The youth said no more, and, after placing the food on the floor at my side, returned up the corridor, taking the light with him. Twice a day the youth came to my cell with food, and delivered the same message from Zat Arras. I tried to engage him in conversation on other matters, but he would not talk.

For months I thought about how to inform Carthoris of my whereabouts. For months I scraped on a single link of my chain hoping to wear it through. Once free I would follow the youth back through the winding tunnels to a point where I could make a break for liberty.

I was consumed with anxiety about Dejah Thoris and the expedition to rescue her. I knew that Carthoris would not let the matter drop, but as far as I knew, he might also be a prisoner.

I knew that the spy had heard our conversation about a new Jeddak, and just a few minutes before we had discussed the plan to rescue Dejah Thoris. All four of my friends and partners might be prisoners or the victims of assassins.

I had to make one more effort to learn something from the youth. I noticed that he was a handsome fellow, about the size and age of Carthoris. I had also noticed that his shabby trappings did not match his dignified and noble bearing. I would use these observations with him on his next visit.

"You have been very kind to me during my imprisonment here," I said to him, "and since I have but a short time to live, I wish to give you a gift of appreciation for all that you have done to make my life bearable.

"You have brought my food each day, seeing that it was pure and of sufficient quantity. You have never tried to insult or harm me. You have been courteous and considerate and that prompts my feeling of gratitude.

"In the guardroom at my palace are many fine trappings. Go there and select the harness that most pleases you and it will be yours. All I ask is that you wear it, so I will know that my wish has been realized. Tell me that you will do it."

The boy's eyes lit up with pleasure as I spoke, and I saw him glance from his rusty trappings to the magnificence of my own. For a moment he stood in thought before he spoke, and for that moment my heart stopped—so much was riding on his answer.

"If I went to your palace with such demand, they would laugh at me and throw me into the street. No, it cannot be, though I thank you for the offer. Of course, if Zat Arras even dreamed that I contemplated such a thing he would cut my heart out."

"There will be no harm in it, my boy," I urged. "By night you may go to my palace with a note from me to Carthoris, my son. You can read the note before you deliver it, so you will know that it contains nothing harmful to Zat Arras. My son will be discreet and no one but us three will know. It is such a simple and harmless act that it would be condemned by no one."

He stood silently in deep thought . . . and I added, "There is also a well made jeweled dagger which I took from a northern Jeddak. When you get the harness, see that Carthoris gives the sword to you, too. With the harness and sword there will be no more handsomely outfitted warrior in all Zodanga.

"Next time you come here bring writing materials and within a few hours we'll see you garbed in a style befitting your birth and carriage."

Still in thought, and without speaking, he turned and left. I could not guess what his decision might be, and for hours I sat fretting. If he accepted a message to Carthoris it would mean that Carthoris still lived and was free. If the youth returned wearing the harness and the sword, I would know Carthoris had received my note and that he knew that I still lived.

I was excited when I heard the youth's approach on his next regular visit. I did not speak beyond my normal greeting but as he placed the food on the floor he also deposited writing materials.

My heart jumped for joy! I wrote a brief order to Carthoris to give Parthak a harness of his selection and the dagger. I put the note on the floor. Parthak picked it up and left without a word.

I estimated I had been in the pits for three hundred days. If anything was to be done to save Dejah Thoris it must be done quickly because those who were chosen by Issus lived only a single year.

The next time I heard approaching footsteps I could hardly wait to see if Parthak wore the harness and the sword. Imagine my disappointment when I saw that it was not him! I stammered, "What has become of Parthak?"

The fellow would not answer, and he quickly deposited my food, turned and retraced his steps to the world above. Days came and went but my new jailer never spoke a word to me.

I could only speculate about Parthak's removal, but knew that it was connected in some way directly with the note. I was no better off than before, I still did not even know if Carthoris was alive.

Thirty days had passed since I gave Parthak the note. Three hundred and thirty days had passed since my incarceration. As closely as I could figure, there remained barely thirty days before Dejah Thoris would be ordered to the arena for the Rites of Issus.

I almost went crazy as that terrible picture forced itself across my imagination but then I heard the sound of my approaching jailer. Now a new and grim determination came to me. I would make one super-human effort to kill my jailer and trust fate to lead me safely to the outer world.

With the thought came instant action. I threw myself on the floor of my cell in a distorted posture, as though I were dead. When the jailer stooped over me I would grab him by his throat with one hand and smash him with my chain.

The doomed man came nearer and nearer and I heard him halt close to me. There was a muttered exclamation, and then a step as he came to my side. I felt him kneel down beside me. My grip tightened on the chain as he leaned close to me. I had to open my eyes to find his throat, grab it, and strike a blow all at the same instant.

The thing worked just as I had planned. So brief was the interval between the opening of my eyes and the fall of the chain that I could not check it, though at that instant I recognized my son, Carthoris!

God! What cruel and awful fate had worked to such a frightful end! What chain of circumstances had led my boy to my side at this one particular minute of our lives when I could strike him down and kill him? He fell on top of me and knocked my head against the floor. My vision blurred as I sank into unconsciousness next to the body of my only son.

When I awoke it was to feel a cool, firm hand pressed on my forehead. For an instant I did not open my eyes. But then came the recollection of my last conscious act, and I feared to see what might be lying beside me. I wondered who it was touching me. Carthoris must have had a companion come with him. Well, I must face the inevitable, so why not now, and with a sigh I opened my eyes.

Leaning over me was Carthoris, a vivid bruise on his forehead where the chain had struck, but alive, thank God, alive! There was no one with him. Reaching out my arms, I hugged my boy, and if there ever was a prayer of gratitude, it was there beneath the crust of Mars in that awful pit as I thanked the Eternal Mystery for my son's life.

"How did you get here?" I asked, mystified that he had found me without a guide.

"It was by the youth, Parthak. Until he came for the harness and sword, we thought that you were dead. I read your note and gave Parthak his harness and brought him the jeweled dagger. But the minute that I fulfilled your promise my obligation to him ceased. I then tied him up and questioned him, but he would give me no information as to your whereabouts. He was intensely loyal to Zat Arras.

"Finally I gave him a choice between his freedom and the pits beneath our palace—the price of freedom to be full information as to where you were imprisoned and directions which would lead us to you; but still he maintained his silence. I had him thrown in our pits, where he still resides.

"No threats of torture or fabulous bribes would move him. His only reply to our demands was that when he died he would not die as a traitor.

"Finally, Xodar, who is a crafty fiend, evolved a plan where we might trick the information out of him. And so I had Hor Vastus harnessed in the metal of a Zodangan soldier and chained in Parthak's cell. For fifteen days the noble Hor Vastus has languished in the darkness of the pits, but not in vain. Little by little he won the confidence and friendship of the Zodangan. Today, Parthak revealed the place where you were imprisoned.

"It took me just a short time to locate the architectural plans for the pits of Helium among your official papers. To get to you was a more difficult matter. While I easily came to the pit entrance at Zat Arras' palace, I found a

Zodangan soldier on guard. I left him there, but his soul was no longer with him.

"And here I am, just in time to be nearly killed by you," he ended, laughing.

As he talked, Carthoris worked at the lock, and I soon stood up, freed from the irons I had chafed in for almost a year. He brought a sword and a dagger for me, and we set out on the return journey to our palace.

Some half-hour later we came to the pits beneath our own palace, and soon we emerged into the audience chamber where we found Kantos Kan, Tars Tarkas, Hor Vastus, and Xodar. No time was lost in recounting my imprisonment. What I desired to know was how well the plans we had laid nearly a year ago had been carried out.

"It has taken much longer than we had expected," replied Kantos Kan. "The fact that we had to maintain secrecy has handicapped us terribly. Zat Arras' spies are everywhere. Yet, we believe no word of our plans has reached the villain's ear.

"A fleet of a thousand battleships is stationed at Hastor and each is equipped to navigate the air and water of Omean. On each battleship there are five ten-man cruisers, and ten five-man scouts, and a hundred one-man scouts; all fitted with both air and water propellers.

"Nine hundred troopships, and their escorts

are at Thark awaiting the green warriors of Tars Tarkas. Seven days ago all was ready, but we waited for your rescue so you could command the expedition, my Prince."

I asked Tars Tarkas, "Why did the men of Thark not take action against you after you admitted you returned from the River Iss and the Valley Dor?"

"They sent a council of fifty chieftains to talk with me. We are a just people, and when I told them the entire story they agreed that their action toward me would be guided by the action of Helium toward John Carter. In the meantime I was to resume my throne as Jeddak of Thark so I could negotiate with neighboring hordes to make up the land forces of the expedition. I have done that which I agreed. Two hundred and fifty thousand fighting men, gathered from the ice cap of the north to the ice cap of the south, fill the city of Thark. They are ready to sail for the Land of the First Born when I give the word. All they ask is the loot they take and transportation to their own territories when the fighting is over. I am done."

"And you, Hor Vastus," I asked, "what has been your success?"

"A million fighting-men from Helium man the battleships, the transports, and the escorts," he replied. "Each is sworn to loyalty and secrecy."

"Good!" I cried. "Everyone has done his

duty! Now, Kantos Kan, let us go to Hastor and get under way!"

"We should lose no time, Prince," replied Kantos Kan. "Already the people of Hastor are asking questions. I have no doubt that some word of it has reached Zat Arras. A cruiser is waiting at your dock; let us leave at—" A fusillade of shots from the palace gardens just outside cut short his words.

We rushed to the balcony in time to see a dozen members of my palace guard disappear in the shadows in pursuit of someone. Directly beneath us a handful of guardsmen were stooping above a prostrate form. We ordered them to bring it into the audience chamber. When they stretched the body at our feet we saw that it was that of a red man in the prime of life—his metal was a plain, common soldier design.

"Another of Zat Arras' spies," said Hor Vastus.

"So it would seem," I replied with some hesitation.

"Wait!" said Xodar. "If you will allow me, Prince, may I have a cloth and a little thoat oil?"

I nodded to one of the soldiers, who quickly brought them to Xodar. He kneeled beside the body, dipped the cloth in the oil and rubbed for a moment on the dead face. He turned to me with a smile, pointing to his work. I looked and saw that where Xodar had applied the oil the face was white, as white as mine. Xodar then seized the black hair of the corpse and with a sudden wrench tore it all away, revealing a hairless dome.

"A Thern!" whispered Tars Tarkas.

"Worse than that, I fear," replied Xodar. "But let us see."

He cut a pouch off the Thern's harness, opened it and took out a gold headband set with a large gem—a perfect mate to the one I had taken from Sator Throg.

"He was a Holy Thern," said Xodar. "It is fortunate that he did not get away."

The officer of the guard entered the chamber.

"My Prince," he said, "I have to report that this fellow's companion escaped us. I think that some of the men at the gate may have helped. I have arrested them all."

Xodar handed him the thoat oil and cloth and said, "Use this to discover the spies."

A half-hour later the officer reported in. This time it was to confirm our fears—half the guards at the gate were Therns disguised as red men.

"Come!" I cried. "We must lose no time. We leave for Hastor at once. If the Therns stop us at the edge of the ice cap it may wreck all of our plans for the expedition."

Ten minutes later we were speeding through the night toward Hastor, prepared to strike the first blow for Dejah Thoris.

The Air Battle

Two hours after leaving my palace at Helium, Kantos Kan, Xodar, and I arrived at the city of Hastor. Carthoris, Tars Tarkas, and Hor Vastus had gone on directly to Thark on another cruiser. There they would load up the troop transports, get under way immediately and move south. The fleet of battleships would overtake them on the morning of the second day.

At Hastor we found everything ready. Kantos Kan had planned every detail of the campaign so well that within ten minutes of our arrival the first of the fleet had soared aloft. One after another the rest of the ships floated gracefully out into the night to form a long, thin line stretching for miles toward the south.

It was not until after we entered our cabin that I thought to ask the date, for up to now I was not positive how long I had been imprisoned. When I was told, I realized that I had not estimated my time in the cell correctly. Three hundred and sixty-five days had passed—it was too late to save Dejah Thoris!

The expedition was no longer one of rescue but of revenge. I did not tell Kantos Kan the terrible fact that the Princess of Helium might not be alive when we got there. She might already be dead because I did not know the exact date she first viewed Issus.

Why should I burden my friends with my added personal sorrows—they had shared enough of them in the past. I would keep my grief to myself, and so I said nothing about the fact that we might be too late. The expedition still could do much good if it only taught the people of Barsoom the facts about their religion. If the expedition could open the Valley Dor to colonization by the red men it would accomplish much. Even in the Land of Lost Souls between the Mountains of Otz and the ice barrier there were many broad areas of potential farmland.

Here at the bottom of this dying world was the only naturally productive area on its surface. Here alone were dews and rains, an open sea, and plenty of fresh water. But all this was the stamping ground of fierce beasts and the wicked remnants of two once powerful races. They barred all the other millions of the planet from this garden of plenty. If I could succeed in breaking down the barrier of religious superstition that kept the red race from this place it would be a fitting memorial to the virtues of my princess. I would serve Barsoom again and the death of Dejah Thoris would not have been in vain.

On the morning of the second day we spotted the fleet of transports and soon were near enough to exchange signals. Tars Tarkas reported all was well with the transports. The battleships passed through to take an advanced position, and the combined fleets raced through the skies until we spotted the ice cap. We then slowed down and reduced our altitude, hugging the surface to prevent detection.

Far in advance a long thin line of air scouts protected us from surprise, while a smaller number guarded the flanks and brought up the rear. We went toward Omean in this formation for several hours. One of our scouts returned from the front to report that the cone-like summit of the entrance to Omean was in sight. At the same time another scout from the left flank came racing toward the flagship.

The scout's speed warned of his information's importance. Kantos Kan and I waited for him on the bridge. Scarcely had his tiny flier come to rest on the landing-deck when he was running up to where we stood.

"There is a large fleet of battleships advancing from the southeast, my Prince," he cried. "There are several thousand and they are advancing directly at us."

"The Thern spies were not at the palace of John Carter for nothing," said Kantos Kan. "Your orders, Prince?"

"Dispatch ten battleships to guard the entrance to Omean. Their orders are to allow nothing to enter or leave the shaft. That will bottle up the fleet of the First Born.

"Direct the battleships into a V formation with the point heading directly south-east. Order the transports, surrounded by their escorts, to follow closely in the wake of the battleships until the point of the V has entered the enemies' line. The V must then open outward and the battleships of each leg engage the enemy and drive them back to make a lane. The transports and their escorts will race through the lane and hold a position above the temples and gardens of the Therns.

"The green troops will then land and teach the Holy Therns a lesson in warfare. It had not been my intention to be distracted from the main issue of the campaign, but we must conquer the Therns or there will be no peace for us while our fleet remains near the Valley Dor."

Kantos Kan saluted and delivered my instructions to his waiting aides. Immediately, the formation of the battleships changed and the ten that were to guard the entrance to Omean were speeding toward their destination. The troopships and escorts were soon closing up in preparation for the spurt through the lane.

The order of full speed ahead was given, the fleet raced through the air, and in another moment the ships of the enemy were in full view. They formed a ragged line three ships deep across the horizon as far as the eye could see. So sudden was our onslaught that they had no time to prepare for it. We were as unexpected as lightning from a clear sky.

Every phase of my plan worked splendidly. Our huge ships mowed their way through the line of Thern battlecraft; then the V opened up and a broad lane appeared. The transports raced toward the temples of the Therns. Before the Therns knew it, a hundred thousand green warriors were pouring through their courts and gardens. A hundred and fifty thousand others leaned out from the transports to direct their almost uncanny marksmanship at the Thern soldiers that manned the ramparts.

Now the two great fleets came together in a titanic struggle far above the fiendish din of battle in the gardens below. Slowly the two lines of Helium's battleships rejoined and then formed the circle that is the characteristic of Helium naval warfare.

Our battleships moved around the circle at high speed so that each one presented a difficult target to the enemy. Broadside after broadside was delivered as each vessel came in line with the enemy ships. The enemy tried to break up our formation, but it was like trying to stop a buzz saw.

From my position on the deck I saw many of the enemy's ships take the awful, sickening dive to its total destruction. Slowly we maneuvered our circle of death until we hung over the gardens where our green warriors were engaged. The order was passed down for them to get back on the transports. Then those ships rose to a position inside the circle.

In the meantime the Therns' fire had practically stopped. They had had enough of us and were only too glad to let us go on our way. But our escape was not to be so easy, for scarcely had we started toward the entrance to Omean when we saw a heavy black line at the horizon. It could be nothing but another fleet of war!

We did not know who they were but Kantos Kan received a radio message which he read and then handed to me.

It read, "Kantos Kan, surrender, in the name of the Jeddak of Helium, for you cannot escape," and was signed, "Zat Arras."

The Therns must have intercepted the message almost as soon as we got it, for they started up the battle again when they realized that we were soon to be set upon by other enemies.

Before Zat Arras had approached near enough to fire a shot we were hotly engaged with the Thern fleet again and as soon as he got near he too commenced to pour a terrific barrage of heavy shot into us. Ship after ship reeled and staggered into uselessness beneath the pitiless fire that we were taking. The battle could not last much longer. I ordered the transports to descend again into the gardens of the Therns.

"Destroy them all," was my message to my green allies, "by night I want no one left alive to avenge your wrongs."

Amid all this I looked up and saw the ten battleships that had been ordered to hold the shaft of Omean returning at full speed. They were firing their stern cannons while being chased by a hostile fleet! Well, it seemed our expedition was doomed. I feared that none of us would make it back across that dreary ice cap. How I wished that I could face Zat Arras with my sword for just an instant before I died! It was he who had caused our failure.

As I watched the ten ships approach I saw what was chasing them. For a moment I could not believe my eyes, but finally I was forced to admit the worst disaster possible had happened— the attacking fleet was none other than the fleet of the First Born. It should have been safely bottled up in Omean!

What a series of disasters! What horrible fate hung over me that I was stopped on every path in my search for my lost love! Could it be possible that the curse of Issus was on me? I did not believe it, and, throwing back my shoulders, I ran to the deck below to join my men. The remainder of my crew were repelling boarders from one of the Thern craft that had grappled us broadside. In the wild lust of hand-to-hand combat my hopeful attitude returned. And as Thern after Thern went down beneath my blade, I could almost feel that we would win in the end.

The men were inspired by my presence and they fell upon the luckless Therns with such ferocity that within a few moments we had turned the tables. A second later as we swarmed their decks I had the satisfaction of seeing their commander take the long leap from the bows of his vessel in a token of surrender and defeat.

I then joined Kantos Kan. He had been watching what had taken place on the deck below, and it seemed to have given him a new thought. Immediately he passed an order to one of his officers, and the colors of the Prince of Helium broke from every point of the flagship. A great cheer arose from the men of our own ship, a cheer that was taken up by every other vessel of our expedition as they in turn broke out my colors.

Then Kantos Kan played his last card. A signal was strung aloft on the highest point of the flagship. A signal seen by fighting men on all the ships engaged in that fierce struggle: "Men of Helium rally around the Prince of Helium against all his enemies!" After a pause, my colors broke out on one of Zat Arras' ships. Then they showed on another and another. On some enemy ships we could see fierce battles waging between the Zodangan warriors and the fighters of Helium, but eventually the colors of the Prince of Helium floated above every ship that had followed Zat Arras—all except his flagship.

Zat Arras had brought five thousand ships. The sky was black with the remaining three enormous fleets. It was Helium against the field now, and the fight had settled into countless individual duels. There could be little maneuvering of ships in that crowded, fire-split sky.

Zat Arras' flagship was close to my own. I could see the thin features of the man from where I stood. His Zodangan crew was pouring broadside after broadside into us and we were returning their fire with equal ferocity. The two vessels came closer and closer until only a few yards separated us. Grapplers and boarders lined the rails. We were prepared for the final death struggle with our hated enemy.

There was only a yard between the two ships as the first grappling irons were hurled. I rushed to the deck to be with my men as they boarded. Just as the vessels came together with a slight shock, I forced my way through the lines and was the first to spring onto the enemy deck. A yelling, cheering, cursing throng of Helium's best fighting-men poured after me. Nothing could withstand them.

Down went the Zodangans before that surging tide, and as my men cleared the lower decks I ran up to the forward deck to face Zat Arras.

"You are my prisoner!" I cried. "Yield and you shall have mercy!"

For a moment I could not tell whether he would accept my demand or face me with drawn sword. For an instant he stood hesitating, and then he threw down his arms and rushed to the far side of the deck. Before I could catch him he leaped over the rail into the depths below.

And thus Zat Arras, Jed of Zodanga, came to his end.

On and on went that strange battle. The Therns and blacks had not joined forces against us. Wherever a Thern ship met a ship of the First Born a fierce battle erupted, and in this I thought I saw our salvation. I passed the word that all our vessels were to withdraw from the fight as rapidly as possible, taking a position to the west and south of the combatants. I also sent an air scout down to the green men fighting in the gardens below with orders to return to their ships and rejoin us.

My commanders were further instructed that when engaged with an enemy to draw him toward a ship of his other enemies, and by careful maneuvering to force the two to engage. The commander was then to withdraw and let them fight it out. This strategy worked well, and just before the sun went down I had the satisfaction of seeing my fleet gathered nearly twenty miles southwest of the still raging battle between the therns and First Born.

I now transferred Xodar to another battleship and sent him with all the transports and half of the battleships directly to the Temple of Issus. Carthoris and I, with Kantos Kan, took the remaining ships and headed for the entrance to Omean.

Our plan was to attempt to make a combined assault on Issus at dawn. Tars Tarkas with his green warriors and Hor Vastus with the red men, guided by Xodar, were to land in the gardens of Issus while Carthoris, Kantos Kan, and I were to lead our smaller force from the Sea of Omean through the pits and attack the temple from below.

At the mouth of the shaft we got into attack formation and then, with the flagship, I dropped into the black depths, while one by one the other vessels followed me.

We had decided to risk everything on the chance that we would be able to reach the temple by the subterranean way and so we left no guard of vessels at the shaft's mouth. For our entrance into Omean, we depended on its boldness, believing that it would take some time before the First Born on guard there would realize that it was an enemy and not their own returning fleet that was entering the vault of the buried sea.

And such proved to be the case. In fact, four hundred of my fleet of five hundred rested safely on the Sea of Omean before the first shot was fired. The battle was short and hot, but the First Born, in their false sense of security, had left only a handful of obsolete ships to guard their harbor.

Carthoris suggested that we tow some captured enemy ships to the shaft and wedge a few of them in the tunnel. Then we turned on the buoyancy rays of a few others and let them rise by themselves to further block the passage.

We now felt that it would take quite a while before the returning First Born could reach the surface of Omean, and that we would have ample time to get to the passages that lead to Issus. One of the first steps I took was to capture the island of the submarine, which we overran and occupied with little resistance from its guards. I found the submarine in its pool, and placed a strong guard around the boat and on the entire island. I waited there for Carthoris and the others.

Among the island's prisoners was Yersted, commander of the submarine. He recognized me from the trips that I had taken with him during my captivity.

"How does it feel to have the tables turned? To be prisoner of your old captive?" I asked him.

He smiled, a very grim smile loaded with hidden meaning, and said, "It will not be for long, John Carter. We have been expecting you and we are prepared."

"So it would appear, for you were all ready to become my prisoners with hardly a blow struck on either side."

"The fleet must have missed you," he said, "but it will return to Omean, and then it will be a very different matter."

"I do not know that the fleet has missed me yet," I said, but of course he did not grasp my meaning, and only looked puzzled.

"Do many prisoners travel to Issus in your submarine, Yersted?"

"Yes, most of them," he agreed.

"Do you remember one whom men called Dejah Thoris?"

"Yes, very well indeed, for her great beauty, and then, too, for the fact that she was wife to John Carter. And they say that Issus remembers her as the wife of one and the mother of another who raised their hands against the Goddess of Life Eternal."

I shuddered at the thought of revenge that Issus might take on Dejah Thoris for the sacrilege of her son and husband.

"And where is Dejah Thoris now?" I asked, knowing that he would say the words I most dreaded. But I loved her so much that I could not stop from hearing even the worst about her fate.

"Yesterday the monthly Rites of Issus were held," replied Yersted, "and I saw her sitting in her accustomed place at the foot of the goddess."

"What," I cried, "she is not dead?"

"Why, no," he replied, "it has not been a year since she gazed upon the divine glory of the radiant face of—"

"Not a year?" I interrupted.

"Why, no," insisted Yersted. "It cannot have been but three hundred and seventy or eighty days."

Suddenly it dawned on me! I had been so stupid! Why had I forgotten the large difference in the length between Martian and Earth years? The ten Earth years I had spent on Barsoom previously had encompassed only five years and ninety-six days of Martian time. Martian days are forty-one minutes longer than ours, and a Martian year numbers six hundred and eighty-seven days.

I am in time! I am in time! The words surged through my brain again and again, until at last I must have voiced them audibly, for Yersted shook his head.

"In time to save your princess?" he asked, and then without waiting for my reply, "No, John Carter, Issus will not give up her own. She knows that you are coming, and before any enemy foot is set inside the Temple of Issus, Dejah Thoris will be put away for ever with no hope of rescue."

"You mean that she will be killed?" I asked.

"No, not killed . . . but something far worse," he replied. "Have you ever heard of the Temple of the Sun? They will imprison her there. It is located far inside the inner court of the Temple of Issus, a little temple with a thin high spire that towers far above the minarets of the larger temple that surrounds it. Beneath the temple, deep in the ground, are many hundreds of circular imprisonment chambers, one below another. A single corridor, cut through the solid rock, leads to each chamber.

"The entire Temple of the Sun revolves once every year and only once each year does the entrance to each separate chamber line up with the corridor which forms its only link to the outside world.

"Those who Issus does not care to execute outright she imprisons in this place. Food for only a certain number of days is left in the chamber. After the food is consumed the inmates die of starvation.

"This is the way Dejah Thoris will die, and her fate will be sealed by the first enemy foot that enters the Temple of Issus."

So I was to be foiled in my quest—even though I performed miracles and had come within a few moments of being with my divine princess. Now it seemed I was as far from her as when I stood on Earth at the Hudson River.

Through Flood
and Flame

The information from Yersted convinced me
that there was no time to lose. I had to reach the
Temple of Issus secretly before the forces under
Tars Tarkas attacked at dawn. Once inside I was
positive we could overcome the guards and carry
away my princess.

Carthoris and the others joined me and we
started to move our men through the tunnel
from the submarine pool to the pits under the
temple. At the beginning of the end of our quest
we were five thousand strong, all seasoned fighting men of the most warlike red men of Barsoom.

Only Carthoris knew the hidden ways of the
tunnels so we could not divide the party and
attack at different points. He was to lead us all to
a point near the temple's center.

As we were about to leave the pool and enter
the corridor, someone called my attention to the
water in the submarine pool—it was rising!

For a moment I did not see the importance of the rising water. It was Carthoris who realized its full meaning—its cause and reason. He shouted, "Move quickly! The pumps of the Sea of Omean have been stopped. We will drown like rats if we linger here. We must reach the upper levels of the pits before the flood!"

"Lead the way, Carthoris," I cried. "We will follow."

At my command, the youth leaped into the tunnel and the soldiers followed him in good order, each company entering the corridor at the command of its captain.

Before the last company left the chamber the water was ankle deep, and the men were quite nervous. They were not accustomed to water except for the small amounts used for drinking and bathing. The red Martians, though brave and well disciplined, instinctively feared deep or menacing water. I was the last to leave the chamber, and as I followed the rear of the column up the corridor, the water was up to my knees.

The march of the troops through the corridor was rapid but not enough for us to gain on the pursuing tide. As the floor of the passage rose, so did the water. Long before the last of the column could hope to reach the upper pits I was convinced that the waters would overwhelm us, and that half the men would drown.

I saw a corridor off to the side that seemed to

rise at a steep angle. The waters were now swirling around my waist. The men were becoming panic-stricken and something had to be done at once or they would stampede and hundreds would die in this rushing water.

I shouted to the captains ahead of me, "Call back the last twenty-five companies! There is a way of escape here! Turn back and follow me!"

My orders were instantly obeyed and the men came back and dashed into the new tunnel. As the first captain passed the officer saluted and he and his men filed past into the corridor in good order. But soon the water rose and men stumbled, floundered, and went down. Many I put back on their feet again, but it was too much for me. Soldiers were being swept under the torrent, never to rise. At length another captain took a stand beside me. He was a tough soldier, and together we kept the now thoroughly frightened troops in order and rescued many of them as they struggled.

As the last company was filing past, the waters had reached up to our necks, but we held on and stood our ground until the last man reached the safety of the new passageway. Here we found a steep incline and within a hundred yards we reached a point above the waters.

For a few minutes we ran up the steep grade. I hoped this would bring us to the higher level pits that led into the temple but I suddenly heard a cry of "fire" far ahead, followed almost at once by cries of terror. The officers' loud commands attempting to direct their men echoed down the passageway. At last the reports came back to me: "They have set fire to the pits ahead!" "We are hemmed in by flames in front and flood behind!" "Help, John Carter! We are suffocating!" and then a wave of dense smoke swept back that sent us, stumbling and blinded, into a choking retreat.

There was nothing else to do but seek a new escape route. The fire and smoke were to be feared a thousand times over the water, and so I charged up the first gallery that led away from the suffocating smoke. After confirming the passage led upward, I stood to one side while the soldiers ran through on the new way. When the stream of men ceased I was not sure that everyone had made it. To assure myself that no poor devil was left behind, I went up the gallery in the direction of the flames. It was hot and stifling, but at last I reached a point where the fire lit up the corridor enough for me to see that no soldier of Helium remained.

My sense of duty satisfied, I turned and started back. To my horror I found that my retreat in this direction had been blocked—steel grating had been lowered across the corridor cutting off my escape!

The smoke from the fire was forcing me further and further back down the dark corridor toward the waters we had just escaped. Finally I felt the lapping waters at my feet. The smoke was thick behind me. There seemed but one thing to do, and so I moved on down the corridor until the cold waters closed around me, and I swam through utter blackness toward—what?

I swam on, waiting for my head to touch the top of the corridor, which would mean that I had reached the limit of my flight and the point where I must sink forever down to an unmarked grave.

But to my surprise I came to the main corridor, and there was still a breathing space between the surface of the water and the rocky ceiling above. I turned in the direction that Carthoris and the head of the column had passed a half-hour before. On and on I swam, my heart growing lighter at every stroke, for I knew that I was approaching the point where I would feel the solid floor beneath my feet again. Once more my chance would come to reach the Temple of Issus.

A few more strokes brought me to a point where my feet touched the ground, and soon I was racing like mad along the corridor searching for the first doorway that would lead me to Issus. If I could not have Dejah Thoris again I was determined to avenge her death. No life would satisfy me other than that of the fiend who caused such horrible suffering on Barsoom.

Sooner than I had expected I came to an exit

into the temple. To me one point was as good as another—I did not know where any of them led! And so I ran up the short, steep incline and pushed open the doorway at its end.

The portal swung in, and I jumped into the chamber. Its sole occupant lay on a couch, apparently asleep. From the hangings and sumptuous furniture of the room I judged it to be a living room of some priestess, possibly of Issus herself.

At the thought, the blood surged through my veins. What if fortune had been kind enough to place the hideous creature alone and unguarded in my hands? With her as hostage I could force agreement to my every demand. Cautiously I approached. Closer and closer I came, but I had crossed little more than half the chamber when the figure stirred, got up and faced me.

At first an expression of terror spread over her face as she confronted me—then it changed to disbelief—then to hope—and finally to thanksgiving. My heart pounded in my chest as I advanced toward her—tears came to my eyes—and the words that would have poured forth in a torrent choked in my throat. I opened my arms and took into them once more the woman I loved—Dejah Thoris, Princess of Helium.

Victory and Defeat

"John Carter, John Carter, my love, my love,"
she sobbed, as she clung to me with her head on
my shoulder; "I can hardly believe my eyes!
When the girl, Thuvia, told me that you had
returned to Barsoom, I listened, but I could not
understand, for it seemed that such happiness
would be impossible for one who had suffered all
these long years. At last, when I realized that it
was the truth, and then came to know the awful
place in which I was held prisoner, I doubted that
even you could reach me.

"As the days passed, and moon after moon
went by without bringing even the faintest rumor
of you, I resigned myself to my fate. And now
that you have come, I can barely believe it. For an
hour I have heard the sounds of conflict inside
the palace. I did not know what they meant, but
I hoped against hope that it might be the men of
Helium headed by my Prince.

"And tell me, what of Carthoris, our son?"

"He was with me less than an hour ago, my princess," I replied. "It must have been his men you heard battling inside the temple."

"Where is Issus?" I asked suddenly.

Dejah Thoris shrugged her shoulders and said, "She sent me to this room just before the fighting began. She said that she would call for me later. She seemed very angry and somewhat fearful. Never have I seen her act in so uncertain a manner. Now I know that it must have been because she learned that John Carter, Prince of Helium, was approaching to demand an accounting of her for the imprisonment of his princess."

The sounds of conflict, the clash of arms, the shouting and the pounding of many feet came to us from various parts of the temple. I knew that I was needed out there, but I dared not leave Dejah Thoris, and I feared to take her with me into the turmoil and danger of battle.

At last I thought of the pits . . . why not hide her there until I could return and fetch her away from this frightful place? I explained my plan to her. For a moment she clung more closely to me and said, "I cannot bear to be parted from you now, even for a moment. I shudder at the thought of being alone again where that terrible creature might discover me. You do not know her. No one can imagine her cruelty who has not witnessed her daily acts with their own eyes."

"I shall not leave you, then, my princess."

She was silent for a moment and then drew my face to hers and kissed me.

"Go, John Carter," she said. "Our son is there with the soldiers of Helium, fighting for the Princess of Helium. Where they are you should be, too. I must not think of myself now, I must think of them and of my husband's duty. I should not stand in the way. Hide me in the pits and go."

I led her to the door where I had entered the chamber. I held her close and then, though it tore my heart and filled me with a terrible feeling of what might happen, I walked her across the threshold, kissed her once again, and closed the door.

Without hesitating, I ran in the direction of the greatest noise until I came to a fierce struggle. The blacks were massed at the entrance to a chamber where they were attempting to block a body of red men headed toward the inner areas of the temple.

I found myself behind the blacks and charged across the chamber and attacked them from the rear with my sword. As I struck the first blow I shouted a battle cry, "For Helium! Attack! Attack!" And then I rained cut after cut on the surprised enemy while the reds on the other side took heart at the sound of my voice. Shouts of "John Carter! John Carter!" sounded out as they redoubled their efforts before the blacks could recover.

The fight in that room would go down in the annals of Barsoom as a historic memorial to the ferocity of her warlike people. Five hundred men fought there that day, the black men against the red. No man asked quarter or gave it. They fought to determine once and for all their right to live—by the law of survival of the fittest.

I think we all knew that the outcome of this fight would determine the ownership of these lands forever. It was a battle between the old and the new, but not for once did I question the outcome. With Carthoris at my side I fought for the red men of Barsoom and for their total release from the bondage of a hideous superstition.

We surged back and forth across the room until the floor was ankle deep in blood. Dead men lay so thick that half the time we stood on their bodies. As I was fighting near the windows overlooking the gardens I saw an amazing sight.

"Look!" I cried. "Men of the First Born, look!"

For an instant the fighting ceased, and every eye turned where I pointed. What they saw was something no man of the First Born had ever imagined.

Across the gardens, from side to side, stood a wavering line of black warriors, while beyond them and forcing them back toward us was a great horde of green warriors astride their thoats. As we watched, one, fiercer and more terrible than the others, rode forward and shouted commands to his terrible fighters.

It was Tars Tarkas, Jeddak of Thark, and as he lowered his long lance we saw his warriors do likewise. Twenty yards now separated the green men from the black line. There was another command from the great Thark, and with a wild and terrifying battle cry the green warriors charged. For a moment the black line held, but only for a moment—then the fearsome beasts that bore their equally fearsome riders passed completely through.

After them came company after company of red men. The green horde broke to surround the temple, the red men charged for the interior, and we turned to continue our interrupted battle; but our foes had vanished.

My first thought was of Dejah Thoris. Calling to Carthoris that I had found his mother, I started on a run toward the chamber where I had left her, with my boy close beside me. After us came those of our force who had survived the bloody conflict.

The moment I entered the room I saw that someone had been there since I left. A silk lay on the floor that had not been there before. There was also a dagger and several metal ornaments strewn about as though torn off in a struggle.

But worst of all, the door leading to the pits where I had hidden my princess was ajar.

With a bound I smashed it open and rushed in. Dejah Thoris had vanished. I called her name again and again, but there was no response. I do not recall what I said or did, but I know that for an instant I was seized with the rage of a maniac.

"Issus!" I cried. "Issus! Where is the goddess? Search the temple for her, but let no man harm her but me. Carthoris, where are her apartments?" I barked.

"This way," cried the boy, and, without waiting to see if I heard him, he dashed off at breakneck speed into the bowels of the temple. As fast as he went, however, I was still beside him, urging him on to greater speed.

At last we came to a large carved door and forced it open. Inside, we saw the scene I had witnessed before—the throne of Issus, with the reclining slaves and the ranks of her soldiers.

We were on them so quickly we did not even give the men a chance to draw their weapons. With a single cut I struck down two in the front rank. And then by the mere weight and momentum of my body, I rushed completely through the two remaining ranks and dashed up onto the dais beside the throne.

The repulsive creature, squatting there in terror, attempted to escape and leap into the hidden trapdoor behind her. But this time I was not to be outwitted by any such trick. Before she moved I had grabbed her by the arm, and then, as I saw the guard starting to rush me from all sides, I whipped out my dagger. Holding it close to that vile throat, I ordered them to halt, "Back! Get back! The first foot that is planted on this platform sends my dagger into this foul heart!"

For an instant they hesitated. Then an officer ordered them back, while from the outer corridor came at least a thousand red men under Kantos Kan, Hor Vastus, and Xodar.

"Where is Dejah Thoris?" I cried to the thing in my hands.

For a moment her eyes roved wildly around the scene. I think that it took a moment for the situation to make an impression on her—at first she could not comprehend that the temple had fallen to the assault of men of the outer world. When she did, there must have come a terrible realization of what it meant to her—the loss of power—humiliation—the exposure of the fraud which she had for so long played on her own people.

There was just one thing needed to complete the reality of the picture she was seeing, and that was added by the highest noble of her realm—the high priest of her religion—who intoned, "Issus, Goddess of Death, and of Life Eternal, arise in the might of thy righteous wrath and with one single wave of thy omnipotent hand strike dead thy enemies! Let not one escape. Issus, thy people depend upon thee. Daughter of the Lesser Moon, only thou art all-powerful. Only thou canst save thy people. We await thy will. Strike!"

And then she went mad. A screaming, gibbering maniac struggled in my grasp. It bit and clawed and scratched in impotent fury. And then it laughed a terrible laughter that froze our blood. The slave girls on the dais shrieked and cowered away. The thing jumped at them and gnashed its teeth and then spat on them from foaming lips. God, but it was a horrid sight.

Finally, I shook the thing, hoping to bring it to rationality.

"Where is Dejah Thoris?" I yelled in her face.

The awful creature in my grasp mumbled for a moment, then a gleam of cunning shot into those hideous, close-set eyes.

"Dejah Thoris? Dejah Thoris?" and that shrill, unearthly laugh pierced our ears once more.

"Yes, Dejah Thoris—I know. And Thuvia, and Phaidor, daughter of Matai Shang. They each love John Carter. Ha-ha! They will meditate inside the Temple of the Sun for a year, but before the year is finished there will be no more food for them. Ha-ha-ha!" and she licked the froth from her cruel lips. "There will be no more food—except each other. Ha-ha! Ha-ha!"

The horror of the suggestion nearly paralyzed me. My princess was condemned to this

awful fate by the creature within my power. I
trembled in my rage. As a terrier shakes a rat I
shook Issus, Goddess of Life Eternal.

"Countermand your orders!" I cried. "Recall
the condemned. Quickly or you die!"

"It is too late. Ha-ha! Ha-ha!" and then she
started her gibbering and shrieking again.

Almost of its own volition, my dagger flew
up above that putrid heart. But something stayed
my hand, and I am now glad that it did. It would
be a terrible thing to have struck down a woman
with my own hand. But a more fitting fate
occurred to me for this false deity.

"First Born!" I cried, turning to those in the
chamber. "You have seen the impotency of Issus!
Issus is no god. She is a cruel and wicked old
woman, who has deceived you for ages. Take her!
John Carter, Prince of Helium, will not contam-
inate his hand with her blood," and with that I
pushed the raving beast from the platform of her
throne into the waiting clutches of her betrayed
and angry people. A short time before, the whole
world had worshipped her—and now the First
Born would reward her crimes with swift and
bloody justice.

Spying Xodar among the officers of the red
men, I called him to lead me to the Temple of the
Sun, and, without waiting to learn what fate the
First Born would give to their goddess, we
rushed from the chamber.

THE GODS OF MARS **239**

Xodor led us through the inner chambers of the temple until we stood in the central court—a circular space paved with marble of exquisite whiteness. In front of us rose a spectacular golden temple, inlaid with diamond, ruby, sapphire, turquoise, emerald, and the thousand other gems of Mars.

"This way!" cried Xodar, leading us toward the entrance to a tunnel that opened in the courtyard beside the temple. Just as we were descending, we heard a deep-toned roar from the Temple of Issus, and a messenger ran up to us through a nearby gate, shouting, "The blacks have set fire to the temple! It is burning in a thousand places. Go quickly to the outer gardens or you are lost!"

As he spoke we saw smoke pouring from a dozen windows looking out on the courtyard, and far above the main temple hung an ever-growing pall of smoke.

"Go back! Go back!" I cried to those who had accompanied me. "Point the way, Xodar! Point the way and leave me. I will reach my princess!"

"Follow me, John Carter," was his only reply, and without waiting he dashed down into the tunnel. I ran at his heels until at last he led me toward a chamber in the distance.

A gate with massive bars blocked our progress into the chamber, but through it I saw her—my incomparable princess, and with her were Thuvia and Phaidor. When she saw me she rushed toward the bars that separated us. Already the chamber had turned so far that only a portion of the opening could be seen. Slowly the opening was closing. In a short time there would be but a tiny crack, and then even that would be gone, and for a long Barsoomian year the chamber would slowly revolve until once more the opening in its wall would pass the corridor's end.

But in the meantime what horrible events would go on within that chamber!

"Xodar!" I cried. "Can no power stop this awful revolving thing? Is there no one who holds the secret of this terrible gate?"

"No one, I fear, who we could fetch in time, though I will go and try to find the priest who is keeper of the keys!"

After he left I stood and talked with Dejah Thoris, and she stretched her hand through those cruel bars so I could hold it until the last moment.

Thuvia and Phaidor also came close, but when Thuvia saw that we wished to be alone she withdrew to the far side of the chamber. The daughter of Matai Shang, however, did not take the hint.

"John Carter," she said, "this is the last time that you will see any of us. Tell me that you love me, so that I may die happy."

"The Princess of Helium is the only one I

love," I replied quietly. "I am sorry, Phaidor, but it is as I have told you from the beginning."

She bit her lip and turned away, but not before I saw the black and ugly scowl she aimed toward Dejah Thoris. After that she stood a little way apart, but not so far as I desired, for I had much to tell my long-lost love.

For a few minutes we stood talking quietly. In a short time the opening would be too narrow for even the slender form of my princess to pass. Oh, where is Xodar? Can he not hurry? Above we could hear the faint echoes of a great battle. It was the black and red and green men fighting their way through the burning Temple of Issus.

A draft from above brought the smoke to us. We waited for Xodar as the smoke became thicker and thicker. Then we heard shouting and hurrying footsteps from the far end of the corridor.

"Come back, John Carter, come back!" cried a voice, "The pits are burning!"

In a moment a dozen men broke through the now blinding smoke to my side. There was Carthoris, and Kantos Kan, and Hor Vastus, and Xodar, with a few more who had followed me from the temple court above.

"There is no hope!" cried Xodar. "The keeper of the keys is dead and his keys are not on his carcass. Our only hope is to quench this conflagration and trust to fate that a year will find your princess alive and well. I have brought enough food to last them all for the entire year. When this crack closes no smoke can reach them, and if we hasten to extinguish the flames I believe they will be safe."

As he spoke Xodar had been tossing many tiny cans into the prison cell. The crack was now not over an inch in width. Dejah Thoris stood as close to it as she could, whispering words of hope and courage, and urging me to save myself.

Suddenly beyond her I saw the beautiful face of Phaidor contorted into an expression of malign hatred. As my eyes met hers she spoke.

"John Carter, do not think that you may so lightly cast aside the love of Phaidor, daughter of Matai Shang. Do not hope to hold Dejah Thoris in your arms again. You may wait the long, long year; but know that when the waiting is over it will be my arms which will welcome you—not those of the Princess of Helium. Behold, she dies!"

And as she stopped speaking I saw her raise a dagger, and then I saw another figure. It was Thuvia. As the dagger fell toward my love, Thuvia got between them. A blinding gust of smoke blotted out the tragedy—a shriek rang out, a single shriek, as the dagger fell.

The smoke cleared away, but we stood gazing at a blank wall. The last crevice had closed, and for a long, Martian year that hideous chamber would retain its secret from the eyes of men.

"In a moment it will be too late," cried

Xodar. "There is only a small chance that we can get through to the outer garden. I have ordered the pumps started, and in five minutes the pits will be flooded. We must get above and make a dash for safety through the burning temple."

"Go," I urged them. "Let me stay here beside my princess—there is no hope or happiness anywhere else for me. When they carry her body from that terrible place let them find the body of her lord awaiting her."

I am confused about what happened after that. It seems like I struggled with many men, and I was picked up and carried away. I do not know. I have never asked, nor has anyone else who was there intruded on my sorrow. No one has said anything that might reopen the terrible wound in my heart.

Ah! If I could know just one thing, what a burden would be lifted from my heart! But whether the assassin's dagger reached one or the other, only time will tell.

Afterword

John Carter has been dead twelve years. But as any reader of *A Princess of Mars* knows, death is only a temporary inconvenience to Carter, a Virginia military man, adventurer, and all-around perfect Southern gentleman. In *The Gods of Mars*, the second volume in a series of books about Carter's Martian adventures, our hero cements his reputation as a great warrior, ladies' man, and lover of justice.

Fans of Edgar Rice Burroughs' most famous books, the *Tarzan of the Apes* series, may find that Carter reminds them of Tarzan, the Lord of the Apes. Burroughs specialized in creating characters who are so naturally superior that the men, women, and even animals they encounter instantly accept their leadership. As soon as Tarzan reaches adulthood, he asserts his dominance over the apes and other animals with whom he lives.

Only the evil ones, like the great ape who kills his human father, resist his leadership. Later in his life, when he encounters his fellow humans, his immense physical strength and intelligence instantly win their respect. Women as well are overcome with admiration for Tarzan's physique and his natural courtesy. The woman who becomes his wife, Jane, willingly gives up her educated, civilized suitors in favor of the brawny lord of the jungle.

Like Tarzan, John Carter is a man who is completely—maybe even unbelievably—superior to those around him. Being magically transported to another planet barely fazes him. He instantly masters the language, customs, and weapons of his new home. Time and time again he is thrust into battles where the odds are impossibly against him, and time and time again he triumphs. He is proclaimed a prince of Barsoom, and there are hints that he may eventually become the Barsoomians' supreme leader. Literally every female he encounters (except the loathsome Goddess Issus) falls for him, and he marries the most desirable of them all: the lovely princess Dejah Thoris. Naturally, the boy he fathers is just as handsome, brilliant, talented, and beloved as John Carter himself.

The *Mars* books are sometimes classified as science fiction, but as the above demonstrates, they really fall better into another category:

fantasy. In fact, *The Gods of Mars* and the other books in its series can be described as fantasy in two senses of the word. They have a fantastic setting—the planet Mars (or Barsoom, as Burroughs calls it). Freed from the reality of Earth, Burroughs is able to create a world populated by beautiful red-skinned maidens, savage white apes, and grotesque life-sucking plant men. But they are fantasies in another way as well. They appeal to the reader's tendency to fantasize—to imagine himself as the hero of the story he is reading. And who doesn't enjoy fantasizing that he is a swashbuckling, undefeatable, brilliant and gallant hero? If Burroughs exaggerates to the point of unbelievability sometimes, we forgive him, because his stories provide so much fun in the telling. It's the same kind of breathless, roller-coaster fun we get today from watching an Indiana Jones movie, *Star Wars*, or *The War of the Worlds*.

A fact that's fun to know about *The Gods of Mars* is that it was originally published in 1913 as a serial in *All-Story Magazine*. As any watcher of television soap operas knows, the key to a successful serial is building in lots of cliffhangers so that audiences will come back for the next installment. You'll note that *The Gods of Mars* is overflowing with such suspenseful moments—nearly every chapter ends with John Carter or his friends facing some apparently inescapable danger. And the biggest cliffhanger of them all is saved for the book's end. Burroughs wanted to make sure readers returned for the next book in his Barsoom series: *The Warlord of Mars.*